Praise for the

Soul Bonds

“I highly recommend Sammi and Mitchell's passionate, sexy and intense love story. I'm happy to report that Lynn Lorenz's new supernatural series, *Common Powers*, gets off to a fantastic start with *Soul Bonds*.”

– Marame, *Rainbow Reviews*

“Ms. Lorenz has blended a contemporary story with a paranormal flare that combines to create a fascinating story. The emotional/ psychic link between Sammi and Mitchell was captivating to watch as it unfolded.”

– Teresa, *Fallen Angel Reviews*

Rush in the Dark

“*Rush in the Dark* is a fantastic follow up to *Soul Bonds.* ”

– Ley, *Joyfully Reviewed*

“*Rush in the Dark* is well written, held my attention and kept me entertained, and there was great sex which this author really knows how to write.”

– *Jessewave*

“In this series, the power doesn’t overwhelm…it only enhances the person. [*Rush in the Dark*] also has friendships, mistakes, pain and fear, but what it also has in abundance, is hope for the future.”

– *Literary Nymphs*

LooseId®

ISBN 10: 1-59632-940-8
ISBN 13: 978-1-59632-940-9
RUSH IN THE DARK: COMMON POWERS 2

Originally released in e-book format in September 2008

Cover Art by Anne Cain
Cover Design and Layout by April Martinez

Printed in the U.S.A. by
Lightning Source, Inc.
1246 Heil Quaker Blvd
La Vergne TN 37086
www.lightningsource.com

RUSH IN THE DARK

COMMON POWERS 2

Lynn Lorenz

Chapter One

"Shit, this stinks," Brian muttered as he crouched behind the dumpster in the back alley of the strip mall.

The bottoms of his boots were coated with the unidentifiable fluids that had leaked from the huge steel bin, and he struggled to keep from gagging. He hated these jobs, but they were the bread and butter of a private investigator, and they paid the bills.

The manager of the video game store suspected his employees were cleaning him out, and he needed proof. His corporation had refused any safeguards, like electronic sensors attached to the packages, let alone any sort of video cameras. He was losing a thousand a month in stolen merchandise, and if it didn't stop, he'd lose his job. Desperate, he'd contacted Brian and hired him to do a little surveillance, take some photos, and get the evidence to catch the thieves.

Brian figured the employees, just teenagers, were using the old trick of putting the stolen property in a garbage bag and then taking out the garbage. After they closed up, they'd come back and do a little dumpster diving, retrieve their loot, and be on their way. That's when he'd catch them.

Simple. Straightforward. Easy money.

Except the part about Brian spending his entire Friday night hiding behind the most disgusting dumpster in all of

Houston. Had something died in there? Shit. He'd really have to scrub to get the stench off when he got home, maybe even burn the clothes he wore. And have the interior of his SUV cleaned, too.

On top of that, he'd been unable to shake the too-familiar feeling that something was going to happen tonight. Something important, maybe even life changing.

In a gesture of comfort, he pressed his hand to the Beretta tucked in its holster under his armpit. He'd learned as a kid not to ignore his premonitions. When he got them, they always happened. Always.

A door opened at the other end of the strip. Loud music and a bass beat blared out. Not the door he was waiting for, but he ducked back into the inky blackness between the dumpster and the wall. No sense in anyone seeing him and raising some sort of alarm.

A man exited and let the door shut behind him, cutting off the music. Brian's eyes widened, and all the blood rushed from his head straight to his cock. From the guy's boots, up his long, black denim-clad legs, and over a pair of broad shoulders that would put Brian's to shame, this guy was every inch a cowboy. Shit, he even wore his black Stetson low on his forehead, letting Brian catch only a glimpse of a strong, rugged jaw and corded neck muscles that disappeared beneath a plaid flannel shirt and denim jacket.

As if posing just for Brian, the cowboy leaned against the building and propped the bottom of a boot flat against the wall, emphasizing a muscular thigh. From where Brian sat, he could hear the guy's soft exhale and had to hold back his own sigh of appreciation at the sight.

The cowboy dug in his jeans for a lighter, reached in a pocket of his shirt, and pulled out a pack of cigarettes. After knocking out a smoke, he put it in his mouth and cupped his hand around the end as he flicked the lighter. After the end caught, he sucked the smoke in deep, held it, and then raised his head to blow out a long stream of grey through slightly parted lips.

Shit. Brian's cock grew another inch just watching the way the guy moved, slow, sure, and so fucking sexy. Brian didn't smoke, but damn, if this cowboy didn't make it the hottest thing he'd ever seen.

As the cowboy smoked, Brian raised his digital camera and clicked off several soundless shots of him. They'd make a fine addition to the two cowboy calendars Brian kept next to his bed just in case he ever needed inspiration during the night.

Down the alley, the door opened. Shit. The video store. So caught up in watching the cowboy, Brian nearly forgot what he was there for. Swiveling, he took a few shots of the young man who approached carrying two garbage bags, holding them as if they were really heavy. Brian bet his Justin boots they were loaded with merchandise.

The kid approached the large bin, saw the cowboy, and froze.

The cowboy nodded. "Evening," he rumbled. Damn. He had to rumble, didn't he? Brian loved the sound of a man's deep voice and this one shot tremors straight to his prick.

The kid nodded, then continued to the dumpster and tossed the bags in with a grunt, turned, and headed back. The cowboy's face was hidden in the shadow of his hat, but Brian was sure he watched the kid all the way to the door.

Brian had to come out from behind the dumpster and check the bags, but the cowboy was still there. He glanced at his watch. They'd be locking up in the next few minutes, and then they'd drive around to the alley and pick up the stash. He had to move quickly.

Standing, he stepped out from behind the bin and came around to the front of it.

"Wondered if you're going to spend all night behind that thing," the cowboy drawled in a deep voice as he flicked the remains of his cigarette into the darkness of the alley.

The guy didn't seem very surprised, as if he'd known Brian was back there all the time. But that was impossible. Brian had hidden in a spot that was absolutely black; he'd checked it from the alley before he ever got back there.

All the witty comebacks he was so good at failed him, and he swallowed hard. He shrugged, then leaned over the dumpster and looked in.

The two bags sat out of reach at the back, almost at the bottom. If he wanted them, he was going to have to go in there and get them. With a quick glance back at the man still leaning against the wall, Brian boosted himself up on his arms and swung his legs over the side of the steel bin and into the midst of the garbage.

The bag he landed on burst and his boots were buried in the flotsam and jetsam of a Chinese restaurant. Between the sickening squelch of the contents and the paint-peeling stench, Brian's vision blurred, and his stomach threatened to erupt.

He'd never eat lo mein again.

Great. The only guy he'd seen in two years to pique his interest and stiffen his cock was going to watch him puke. And then dig through garbage. Just fucking great.

A soft chuckle floated on the air. Brian swallowed hard again, clamped his lips shut tight as he held his breath, and bent to the bags. He untied them, pulled a small flashlight from his back pocket, and inspected the contents.

A dozen video games nested in shredded paper. *Bingo.* Brian held the flashlight in his teeth as he pulled out a marker and made an X on the bag. Under florescent light, the X would show. Then he opened the other bag, checked it, and closed it. After marking it, he straightened and felt his back pop.

At thirty-three, he was getting too old for dumpster diving.

He looked up to see the cowboy push back his hat and give Brian the sexiest lopsided smile he'd ever seen. Shit. Was that a fucking cleft in his chin? Despite standing almost knee-deep in garbage, Brian couldn't stop his cock's renewed stiffening.

Strong and rugged was the best description he could come up with in the dim light of the back alley, but Brian didn't need a spotlight to tell him this was one hell of a handsome man.

"Found what you're looking for?" the cowboy drawled, clearly enjoying Brian's odorous predicament.

"Yeah." Brian hopped out and landed on his feet. Looking down at his own boots and the stained bottoms of his jeans, he grimaced. "Shit." He shook his head and looked up to catch the man's smile turn into a wide grin. Brian stifled a groan. He wanted to explore that deep dent in the guy's chin with his tongue.

"I hope you got a good reason to be digging in the garbage."

"I'm a PI, and I'm trying to catch a couple of employees stealing." Brian wiped his hands on his jeans. The stench coming off him made his eyes water. Surely, the cowboy had to smell him from where he stood.

The big man jerked his chin up. "You can keep the photos."

Struggling to keep his face from showing his surprise, Brian said, "What photos?"

"Never mind," he said with a knowing smile.

How the hell he knew Brian had taken pictures of him was beyond Brian's understanding. The man had to have eyes that could see in the dark, like some cat.

They stared at each other in the dimness and squalor of the back alley. From the cowboy's eyes, a jolt of pure lust leaped across the distance. Bypassing Brian's brain, it swept through him and lodged deep in his loins to set his body on fire. He'd never been promiscuous, never fucked anyone in a bathroom, or in the back rooms of gay bars, much less had sex in an alley, but if given the chance with this man, he didn't think he could stop himself from going down on his knees right here and right now.

Hell, his jeans were already ruined.

The cowboy straightened and rubbed the back of his hand across his chin, as if pondering what was going on. Had the stranger been thinking about sex in a dark alley also? Reseating his hat on his head, he gave Brian a glimpse of thick, tawny gold hair.

The door opened. A man leaned out and frowned at the cowboy.

"There you are. We're leaving. John's in a snit and wants to go home. He's pissed that you just got up and left."

"He was boring, and I needed a smoke," he said, his gaze locked with Brian's. There was no apology in his deep voice.

The intensity of their gazes superheated. Brian felt an unmistakable pull toward the man on the other side of the alley, his cock leading the way as it tried to burst through his jeans.

"Come on, then." The man reached out, but before he could touch the cowboy, he'd pushed off from the wall and ambled toward Brian, whose prick was now a thick lump.

"You smell like you tangled with a skunk and lost." His eyes, dark blue if Brian could tell right, smiled at him, but his full lips stayed in a straight line. Reaching into his back pocket, he pulled out his wallet, opened it, and took out a business card.

Hand extended, he offered it to Brian, the small white rectangle held between two long fingers like a playing card. He searched Brian's face as if memorizing it. The moment seemed frozen in time, along with Brian's heartbeat. Time sped up. Brian's heart thudded hard as he took the card.

"Call me." The cowboy turned away, headed back across the alley, and went inside.

The door slammed shut leaving Brian hard as a rock, aching, and alone.

The sound of a car and headlights broke him from his daze. Shoving the card in his pocket, he darted behind the dumpster as the car roared down the alley and pulled to a stop beside the bin.

Brian raised the camera and snapped off a dozen photos as the kid climbed in, retrieved the bags, then climbed out and shoved them in the trunk. He snapped a few more, then sneaked around to the edge of the bin to catch a final shot of the license plate as the door slammed and the car sped off.

Trotting around to the front of the strip mall and over to his car, he got in, flipped open his cell phone, and dialed the police. With the images in his camera, and the marked bags, they'd have enough evidence to prosecute.

Damn, he stank. He got out of the close confines of the car and waited in the humid night air for the cops to show. He'd give them his evidence and let the boys in blue track them down. He already had their names and addresses from the manager, so it shouldn't be hard to find them.

What a night. He closed his eyes and groaned. He'd found the cowboy of his dreams while standing chest deep in a dumpster, digging through rotting garbage, and stinking worse than roadkill. He'd had a feeling about tonight, and once again, he'd been right.

Brian dug into his pocket and looked down at the business card.

Rush Weston

The Double T Ranch.

Brangus Cattle and Quarter Horses.

Spring Lake, Texas

He turned the card over and a phone number was printed across a faded image of horses running in an open field.

Hot damn. He really was a cowboy.

The lights of the Houston PD cruiser swept over Brian. He tucked the card carefully in his wallet, then pushed off the side of his car to greet the officers.

Chapter Two

Rush eased his large frame into the rough-hewn log chair on the front porch of the ranch house, propped his boots on the railing and stared out into the darkness of the night. There were a million stars in the clear sky, and just a sliver of a moon. He closed his eyes, switched to night vision, then opened them.

The old female possum picked its way over the cattle guard five hundred feet up the road and meandered off to its home under the stand of oleanders Rush's mother had planted over twenty years ago. An owl hooted from its perch on the limb of one of the live oaks that lined the long drive down to the highway. At the threat, the possum scurried to its den and disappeared below ground.

In the sharp night air, Rush could smell the cattle in the far pastures and the pungent smells of manure and hay from the horse barn. This was his favorite time, when the hired hands were gone for the day, everything stilled, and just the sounds of nature could be heard.

He pulled out a cigarette, lit it, and inhaled. Letting the smoke out in a long exhale that was more like a sigh, he leaned back and balanced on the rear legs of the chair his daddy had made a lifetime ago. For as long as Rush could remember, it had been his dad's throne here on the porch. Now Rush ruled the Double T from it.

When he was young, his mother would sit in the porch swing with him and his younger brother Robbie nestled on either side of her. Five years had passed since her body had warmed its wooden slats. Almost fifteen since Robbie had sat beside her. Rush hated to look at it, hated to think of taking it down. His dragged his gaze away, tamped down the pain of loss that still tore at his heart, and looked up at the sky.

It'd been nearly five days since he'd seen the man crouched behind the dumpster, and every single night Rush had lain naked in his bed and pulled up the memory of a large masculine body, full lips, deep brown eyes, and wavy brown hair. That image and his hand had been all he'd needed to release his growing sexual tension.

He only ventured into Houston when necessity drove him there, and last Friday had been no exception. There weren't any gay men out here in Spring Lake. Well, none whom he'd ever found, so Rush went to Houston to slake his forbidden appetites.

Standing in that alley, dressed completely in black, the man had oozed sensuality despite being covered in the crap and stink from that dumpster. He'd made Rush's balls tighten, and the ache he'd come to Houston to ease had grown more insistent, more painful. More sweet.

No call again tonight.

What a fool he'd been, thinking that the guy had felt the same hot shot of sexual desire that Rush had. But he didn't think he'd mistaken the look of hunger in the PI's eyes. As he remembered the intensity in those dark eyes, Rush's cock stiffened in his jeans.

Fuck.

He'd been so shaken that he'd blown his opportunity, hadn't even asked for the guy's card or his name or his fucking number, just told him that he stank. Now, there's a real smooth opening line sure to fire a man's passion and sweet talk him into bed.

Rush snorted. Now, the sexy PI was gone, and nothing Rush could do would get him back. He'd even thought about going back to the bar, but it was insane to think the object of his lust would still be hanging around in the alley.

The front legs of the chair hit the floor, along with Rush's boots, and he stood. Leaning against the railing, he took a last drag and flicked the butt out into the night. It landed with the others in front of the hitching rail.

He whistled for the dogs, hunting around somewhere on the vast property, and listened for their barks. Beau and Bandit, two black labs, came bounding around the side of the house and onto the porch.

After giving them each a thorough ear rubbing as they danced around his legs, he opened the screen door, let the dogs dash past him, and went inside. As he locked up, the dogs went to their food bowls in the mudroom off the kitchen. He made his way upstairs to his room, undressed, and stretched out on the bed, His long, thick cock lay warm against his belly and its eye stared at him, as if to say, "You really fucked up this time, Weston."

Another night of jerking off to a memory of the man who made his prick stiffen, his balls ache, and had him coming harder than he had in a long time.

Rush reached for the lube, spread it on his fingers, and closed his eyes.

* * *

"So, there I was, covered in garbage, ready to puke from the stench, and I meet the cowboy of my dreams." Brian sat back and took a sip of coffee from his favorite mug, the words "Cowboy Butts Make Me Nuts" stenciled on the side.

Across the table, his best friend, Mitchell, and Mitchell's life partner, Sammi, looked at each other and then burst into laughter. Sammi cleared the table, gathered the dinner plates, and placed them in the sink.

"Really, Brian, you couldn't come up with a better line than 'What photos?'" Mitchell chuckled.

Brian gave them a sheepish look. "I still don't understand how he saw me in the dark. It was like a cave, pitch black."

Sammi, his hand resting on Mitchell's shoulder, slipped onto his chair. "Maybe he has"— he paused— "you know...powers." His dark eyebrows rose under the curtain of straight ebony bangs that hid one side of his face.

"No way." Brian shook his head.

"Why not? If you can tell what's going to happen before it does, and Sammi and I can hear each other's thoughts and feel each other's emotions, why can't he see in the dark?" Mitchell asked.

"It's not the same." Brian took another sip.

"How?" Sammi looked at him, tilted his head to one side while waiting for Brian's answer.

"I don't know. That would make his powers more physical, I guess. Kind of… animal?" Brian struggled to put his feelings to words.

"That doesn't make it bad, you know. Just different," Mitchell said.

The timer binged.

"Did you call him?" Sammi stood, picked up a potholder, opened the oven, and pulled out the cinnamon rolls he'd baked from scratch for their dessert.

Mitchell inhaled deeply. "Those smell great, babe."

"Sure do. The whole meal was great, Sammi," Brian said. "You're really picking up a lot working with Otis at The Grill."

Sammi transferred the rolls to a plate and then brought it to the table. "Otis has been good to me." He nodded. "I'm learning so much from him. By the time I actually go to culinary school this fall, I won't be so clueless."

Mitchell wrapped an arm around Sammi's waist and pulled the younger man to him. "You're not clueless, just inexperienced, babe."

Sammi leaned in and kissed Mitchell. Their eyes closed, and Brian wondered what feelings and thoughts had passed between the two lovers. Their kiss deepened.

"Hey, guys, get a room!" Brian laughed, happy that his best friend had found someone to love and spend his life with. Now, if Brian could just do the same, the world would be perfect, like those rolls Sammi had just made. Brian snatched one up and placed it on his plate.

It had been almost a week since he'd met Rush Weston in a back alley and every night, he'd jerked off to the memory of the man. He'd even printed out his favorite photo of Rush and left it on his night table, in case he needed it. So far, his memory had served him just fine.

"Call him," Sammi said, not letting it drop. "I know you want to."

"I will." Brian couldn't lie; at this close range, Sammi could read his thoughts.

"When?" Mitchell pressed, as he took a bite of his roll.

"Tonight. I swear." Brian took a gulp of coffee to wash down a bite of roll.

How Rush could have been interested in him, smelling as bad as he did, was a wonder to Brian. Good Lord, the cowboy was Brian's dream man, big, built, and blond. At six two, Brian was taller than average, but Rush had to be six three or four. Even though Brian was a handsome man and usually immaculately dressed, he'd definitively not been at his best that night.

"You promise?" Mitchell pushed.

"I promise. What the hell? Why not? Other than my pride, I don't have much to lose." Brian shrugged.

"Maybe you'll change your life." Sammi gave Brian a knowing smile, making Brian wonder if Sammi's powers were greater than he'd thought.

"Look, Sammi, I wanted to let you know. I have some free time now and I'm going to start working on your case."

Brian looked across into the young man's eyes and watched as hope rose in them.

"Really? You're going to try to find out who I am? That's great." Sammi clutched Mitchell's hand.

"Thanks, Brian. If we can't get Sammi a last name and social security number, his plans for college will never get off the ground," Mitchell said.

"I want to pay you." Sammi sat straighter. "I'm making some money now, and I don't want you to do this for free."

"It's not necessary." Brian tried to wave him away.

"It is. I insist." Sammi's jaw was set, and Brian could see the guy meant it.

"Okay. My rate is twenty bucks an hour, plus expenses." Brian rattled off the number, roughly one-third of his normal price, but Sammi didn't know that. Mitchell did, and he flicked his eyes to Brian's as one eyebrow rose.

"It's a deal. Just let me know how much as you go, so I can budget for it." Sammi nodded.

"I just need some info to get started with," Brian said as he took out his BlackBerry. "Do you remember anything from any of your foster parents or where you lived?"

"I had so many I can't remember them all, and most of them I wanted to forget. I've always been in Houston, as far as I know. When I ran away, they were Don and Jan Ranks, I think, because when I went to school I used their name. But it was a long time ago. Once I got on the streets, I just used Sammi. By the time I fell in with Donovan, I'd forgotten so much from when I was little. Guess I blocked most of it out." Sammi frowned; his dark eyes seemed lost and sad, like those of a kid. At twenty-three, he was part man, part youth, but Brian couldn't deny that Sammi was definitely all sexy.

At the mention of Donovan's name, Mitchell growled. Brian could see the anger in his best friend's eyes. Donovan had run a sex slave ring, and Sammi had been his prize possession until he escaped, met Mitchell in a bar, and they'd fallen in love.

Brian had helped Mitchell rescue Sammi and now they were helping the young man rebuild his life, and that included finding out his real name. Brian couldn't imagine not knowing who he was or what a horror Sammi's life must have been, but he was determined to do whatever it took to find out the truth.

Chapter Three

Brian stepped from the shower, grabbed a towel, and rubbed himself dry. With it slung over his shoulders, he brushed his teeth and gazed into his reflection.

"You're a big coward, Russell."

His reflection nodded back, agreeing. Cowardice was new to him. This reticence about calling Rush was so unlike him. Usually, he leaped into relationships without looking, opened his heart to love that had led ultimately to the breaking of said heart.

There was something monumental about the way he felt about Rush. Something that said if he screwed this one up, he was just a loser, destined to being alone. His premonition about that night changing his life had him spooked like never before.

Even as a kid, when he'd had those flashes of insight, they hadn't scared him. He just knew they would come true. No reason to question it, it just was— like breathing.

As Brian grew up that nonchalance about his power had turned to uncertainty. Why him? What was he supposed to do about it, be some sort of superhero? Go around saving people?

He'd always wanted to be a cop and use this heightened perception to help people, but the sultry summer he turned fifteen, he'd kissed a boy his age and confirmed the whispering fear that he was gay.

At the time, gay cops weren't de rigueur, so even though he'd taken law enforcement courses, he'd majored in civil engineering at the University of Texas and forgot about a career as a cop.

As for love, each of Brian's two lovers had broken his heart and then moved on. From the first time he'd fallen in unrequited love, to the loss of his virginity to an older lover who'd wooed him, fucked him, and then dumped him, the pain he'd felt seemed magnified each time his heart had been broken. Undaunted, he'd kept his hopes up and his heart open and believed one day he'd find the perfect man.

And he did. He would never forget the first time he saw Steve. Brian fell in love in a single moment. Steve was tall, blond, well built, and so sexy.

And he belonged to Brian's best friend, Mitchell.

Mitchell loved Steve and Steve loved Mitchell. Brian loved Steve and Brian loved Mitchell more than a brother. No way on earth would he ever betray Mitchell. So Brian never said a word for the two and a half years Steve had lived with Mitchell.

Then, one rainy night on the interstate, Steve had a flat tire. As he was getting the tire out of the trunk, a drunk driver slammed into the car, tearing Steve's body in two as if he were a rag doll.

Mitchell had been devastated.

Brian had been there for him, while suffering his own numbing loss of a love he'd never known for a man who'd never touched him other than a handshake or a slap on the back.

During the years between then and now, Brian had developed a modest interest in a few men, but nothing lasting had ever come of it. At the advanced age of thirty-three, Brian had had exactly four lovers, and none of them had been the One.

Rush was the One.

Brian was as sure of it as he was the color of his own eyes, that he hated snakes, and that he'd never have to register his guns in Texas. If he blew this, it was over. There would be no more chances for a life lived and spent loving one man. It was a terrifying thought, to spend his life alone and unloved.

There was no choice but to open his heart and take a chance.

Dropping his towel into the hamper, he went to his dresser, opened his wallet, and took out the card.

Rush Weston, The Double T Ranch.

Sitting on the edge of his bed, Brian glanced at the clock. Nine thirty. Was it too late to call the ranch? Didn't cowboys go to bed with the chickens and get up with the rooster? No, these days they had cable and satellite TV.

He picked up his cell phone, flipped the card over, and punched the number in.

After the fourth ring, a deep voice answered, "Hello?"

Brian's stomach did that flip thing. "Is this Rush Weston?"

"It is."

"This is Brian Russell." Brian took a breath. "The guy in the alley Friday night." He winced. At least he hadn't described himself as the man covered in garbage.

"The PI?" Rush's voice rose just a hair.

Brian's stomach flipped again. Shit, he needed to bring that under control. He was like a kid with a crush. "That's me." Great comeback, Russell.

"Did you catch the outlaws?"

"I did. Well, the cops caught them. I just got the evidence."

There was a long stretch of silence. Brian could hear Rush breathing on the other end of the line. His rebellious stomach dropped. That was it. They'd run out of conversation in the first two minutes.

"I didn't think you were going to call," Rush said in a husky breath.

"I should have called sooner. Sorry." Did he need to tell Rush what a coward he'd been and that he'd needed to work up the nerve to call him?

"Been thinkin' 'bout you." Rush's voice lowered, as if it could go any deeper.

"Me, too." Shit. That was lame. "Every night."

He heard the cowboy's long exhale. Was he smoking? Just the memory of Rush smoking that cigarette sent shivers down his spine.

"Same here." Rush was not a man of many words, it seemed.

Brian would have to be the one to get things started. He settled back against the headboard of his bed, his semierect cock lying against his thigh and let out a long sigh, right into the phone.

"Are you in bed? Did I wake you?" He softened his voice.

"I'm in bed, couldn't sleep."

"Thinking about me?" Brian let his voice drop lower.

"Yep." There was a hint of a smile behind that one word.

Brian took a breath, closed his eyes, and jumped. "Shit. Do you know how many times I've jerked off thinking about you, Rush?"

Another long exhale. "'Bout as many times as I've whacked off thinking of you."

Brain laughed softly. "And tonight?"

"Not yet. You?"

"Just about to. Care to join me?"

"Dang it, Brian. You sure know what to say to get a man hard."

"I'm glad." Brian gathered his cock in his hand and gave it a stroke. "Are you touching your cock?"

"Ever since I knew it was you."

Shit. Brian tugged harder, his cock thickening. "I wanted you that night. Thought about fucking you in that alley, but…"

"Not the right time, was it?"

"No. Next time we meet, I'll make sure I smell better."

"You'd get all cleaned up just for me?"

"Just for you. Did you want…?" Brian hated to sound needy, but he wanted to know if Rush had wanted him that night, too.

"If Mike hadn't come out and got me, I might not have let a little thing like the way you smelled stop me."

"Mike? Is he your lover?" Brian felt sick. Of course, a guy like Rush probably had a lover, maybe several.

"No, just a friend. He tried to hook me up with this friend of his that night."

"John? The guy in a snit?"

"You remembered?"

"I spent a long night wondering what you were doing to John that you could have been doing to me." Brian's vivid imagination had tortured him that night.

"I was going to go home with him, but after seeing you, well, I have to admit, he paled in comparison."

"Are you saying I've spoiled you for other men?" Brian felt a quiet thrill.

"Something like that." Rush chuckled.

"You cowboys say the sweetest things."

"Better than telling you that you smelled like a skunk," he said. "Sorry about that, but you had me twisted up in my ropes."

"I did smell like a skunk. Not now. Just got out the shower."

"Naked as a jaybird and twice as sassy?"

"Definitely naked. Sassy? I'm not so sure."

"Got a hard-on for you, Brian. Need some fucking relief, darlin'."

"That night, I thought about doing you in my car."

"Tell me."

"We'd go to my car and get in the front seat. At first, we'd just stare at each other, letting the fire burn between us like it did in the alley."

"You felt that, too?"

"I felt it, and I'm damn glad to know you did, too. So, you reach over, put your hand around my neck, and pull me in for a kiss."

"Are you a good kisser?"

"Want to find out?"

"Can't wait to find out how you taste on my tongue. Do you like to use your tongue?" Rush growled. Brian's balls tightened, and he squeezed his shaft tighter.

"Oh, yeah. I'd like to use my tongue on your dick."

A deep inhale, followed by a long exhale. "So after we kiss, then what?"

"Then, I'd unbutton your jeans. I figure you for a button-fly man."

"Real cowboys only wear button-flys."

"And you're a real cowboy?"

"Damn straight. Got the horse and the six-shooter to prove it." Brian loved the way the cowboy drawled his words. It sent a shiver of desire straight through him.

"So, I'd flick open those buttons, one by one, slow and easy. The whole time your cock is begging to be let out. Tell me about your cock."

"Right now, it's long, thick, and aching for you."

"Just like I imagined it, Rush. I free it and your balls from your pants, but leave the pants tight up around them, so your package is showcased just for me."

"What do I do?"

"You moan like a bitch when I take you in my mouth."

"Fuck, Brian, you just made me harder."

"I suck you, then go back and forth between licking that juicy head and licking your balls."

Harsh breathing filled Brian's ears as he imagined Rush pumping hard on his prick, bringing himself off as he listened.

"Then, you bury your hands in my hair and hold me down. Your hips start moving and you're fucking my mouth, and I'm groaning and you keep driving into me, deep in my throat, but I'm taking every fucking inch of you," Brian rasped, his hips moving as he jerked off in a near frenzy. On the edge of coming, with just a little more, he'd lose it.

"Damn it, darlin', you got me like a pistol. Hot, loaded, and ready to shoot," Rush groaned.

"Then you're exploding into my mouth, hitting the back of my throat, hot and salty and so fucking delicious, I know I'm going to want more of you. I'm swallowing you down, sucking on your dick, getting every last drop of your cum, and you're moaning and calling out my name."

Rush groaned. "Fuck, darlin'. It feels so sweet. Here it comes…" His words were lost in a strangled cry as he came.

Brian cried out as he lost his load, shooting all over his belly. His fingers slid up and down on his cock, spreading his own creamy cum over his dick as he milked himself.

"Rush, oh shit, that was so hot," Brian whispered as he bathed his balls with his jism.

Their harsh panting as they recovered from their orgasms echoed in the phone line.

Brian shuddered and then lowered his voice to a sexy-as-hell whisper. "Did you get my cell phone number, cowboy?"

"Yeah, it's on my phone," Rush breathed.

"Good. Call me." Brian hung up.

He flopped back on the bed and tried to steady himself. He'd just hung up on the man of his dreams, but he'd wanted to leave Rush begging for more. Brian had taken a chance on the move to do just that, to make Rush crave even more of him. He wanted Rush to want him and no one else.

The only problem was now he'd have to wait until Rush called him. Shit. Maybe Rush would make him wait five nights until he called back. Brian groaned. It would serve him right for being such a coward. If he'd gone with his heart, instead of his head, he would have called Rush the next day.

What if he'd made a mistake? What if Rush didn't call back and tonight had been all he'd wanted from Brian? Brian wanted so much more from Rush than a jack-off session over the phone.

He wanted Rush's body. His heart. Everything the man had to give.

Chapter Four

"Hello, gorgeous," Brian said as he leaned against the chest-high wall of the grey cubicle. The black woman he grinned down at paused, flicked her amber eyes up at him, gave a soft *humph*, and then went back to her typing, her long purple nails clattering on the computer's keyboard.

"Hello, yourself." She peered over the half-glasses perched on the end of her nose at her computer. "What do you want?" She frowned at the screen.

"Now, Sheila, what makes you think I want anything? Can't a man just drop in on his favorite woman now and then?" Brian shook his head.

"No, because every time you darken my door you need something. Now, are you sure I'm your favorite woman?" She batted unnaturally long lashes at him. "'Cause I don't mess with no playas."

"Of course you're my favorite."

"You mean, I'm your only," she shot back. Taking her hands off the keyboard, she picked up a huge cup of water and took a sip. "Now, what can the Department of Children's Protective Services do for you today, Mr. PI?"

Brian eyed her large expanse of breasts, like two plump pillows that any man, straight or gay, would be pleased to rest his weary head upon. Sheila Mae Wilkins was his connection at the bureau and a longtime friend. When he'd first hung out his PI shingle, he'd helped her brother, and she'd never forgotten it.

"Well, I'm looking for a man."

"Aren't we all, honey, aren't we all. Don't have no men here, just kids. Did you check the bars?" She laughed loudly at her joke.

"Har-dee-har-har," Brian retorted. "You're a card, Sheila, a card. No, he would have been in the system about eight or nine years ago. He ran away from his foster home at sixteen and fell off the grid. I have the name of his last foster parents, but I've searched for them, and it looks like they're not in the Houston area anymore." They could be anywhere in the U.S. and the Internet search had come up empty. It was just the first of many dead ends Brian was sure he'd hit on this case.

She turned back to her computer, all business. "Let's see what I can find. Not promising anything, though. Our current records only go about five years back, anything more than that, and it's probably been archived."

"Give it a try, anyway. Maybe we'll be lucky."

"What's this 'we'? Maybe you'll get lucky."

"I need some luck, that's for sure."

"You got a name for the kid?"

"Just a first name— Sammi. Possibly Samuel."

"Social security number?"

"Nope. I got nothing, Sheila." He shook his head and gave her his best "poor me" look.

"Naturally." She let out the sigh of the long-suffering government worker. Brian wondered if they had to master it to be hired on as civil servants or if there was a training course.

She typed. Brian waited. She shook her head and typed again. Brian leaned closer to watch the screen. With a soft muttered word or two not used by Christian women, she turned to him.

"Sorry, sugar. My records only go back five years."

"What about the foster parents? Their name is Ranks, Don and Jan."

Again, her long nails clacked over the keyboard. They waited. She sat back and shook her head. "No one by that name in the system."

It figured. Nothing about Sammi had been easy, except how Mitchell had fallen in love with the young man. Sammi was sexy as hell and nothing but trouble.

"How do I get to the archives?" He had no choice but to do this the hard way. Hours of research stacked up in his imagination.

"Well, you take US Highway 290 and head straight up to Austin."

"Austin?" Brian's shoulders slumped. Not that he minded the drive, but navigating the capital city's red tape was a pain in the ass.

"That's right. You can go up there, or fill in some forms here and wait a month or so." She reached into a stack of yellow forms. "You want one?"

"No." Brian sighed. "It's Austin, I guess."

"The old records are pulled off the system; then they're either put on microfiche or optical scanners, depending on what they used at the time. Might even be on the new servers we use for backup now, I'm not sure. You can request the records and view them at our office near the capitol building."

"Have you got a name for me in Austin? Someone who might help me once I get up there?" Brian gave her his best smile.

She laughed at his attempt. "Boy, don't be giving me that sexy grin of yours, flashing those dimples. It may work on your boyfriends, but it won't work on me."

Brian added a wink.

"Aw, now I hate it when you do that. Makes me get all weak-kneed and woozy." Her sarcastic tone wasn't lost on him, and she looked neither weak-kneed nor woozy. She picked up a card, turned it over, and wrote a name down. "When you get there, ask for Roberta. Tell her I sent you. She'll help you find your man."

"Thanks, Sheila, you're a dream. If I was straight..." He gave her a kiss on her mahogany cheek and took the card from her.

"Honey, that's what they all say." She shook her head and went back to her typing.

Brian left. It was already midafternoon, and it would take three hours to get to Austin. He'd just have to drive to the capital first thing in the morning. Wanting to let Sammi know about his progress, he flipped open his cell phone, found Sammi's number, and hit Dial. Since Brian was now being paid for his time, even at a highly reduced rate, Sammi should decide if it was worth it to make the trip.

Sammi answered after a few rings, "Hello? This is Sammi." Brian could hear the clatter of pots, pans and other cooking utensils in the background.

"It's Brian. Can you talk?"

"Sure, hold on." Sammi said something to someone, probably Otis, the old cook he worked for, and then, after a moment, things quieted. "I'm back. What's up?"

"Well, I struck out at CPS, but I really didn't think I'd learn much there. Seems all the data from when you were in the system has been archived and the fastest way to get it is to go to Austin. I could fill out a form and wait for a month or so, but this way we'll know pretty quick."

"Austin?" Brian could hear Sammi's hesitation. "How long will that take?" Twenty bucks an hour was a lot of money for Sammi, who only made six bucks an hour working in the kitchen as a prep cook.

"Three hours up and back, plus the time it takes once I'm there to look through the documents."

Silence as Sammi probably calculated how much that would cost him. Brian was sure it would never occur to Sammi to ask Mitchell for the money. Mitchell loved Sammi and would give it to him in a heartbeat, but Sammi was fiercely independent, refusing to be beholden to anyone and that included finances.

"All right. I need to know as soon as possible. Without that info, I can't even take the GED test, much less think about college." He heard Sammi take a deep breath. "Thanks,

Brian. Really, thanks for everything." Sammi's smile could be felt even through the phone line.

Grinning, Brian hung up. This was the part of his job he loved, doing something for others, helping them. It's why he'd always wanted to be a cop, and why he'd given up working as an engineer to become a private investigator.

He hoped whatever he found out in Austin would lead to discovering who Sammi really was, and perhaps reuniting him with his family, if he had any.

* * *

Brian stepped out of the shower and heard the phone ringing.

"Crap!" He slung himself around the shower door, slipped on the tiles, caught himself on the counter before he went down, and dashed into his bedroom.

His cell phone sat on his bedside table, chirping its urgency. Naked and soaking wet, he launched himself into the air and dove over the bed. As he skimmed the bedspread, he grabbed the phone and slid right off the other side, landing with a hard smack on the wood floor in the jumble of bedspread, sheets, and pillows that followed in his wake.

Flipping the phone open, he gasped, "Hello?" He could hear his own harsh breathing echoing back in his ear. Shit. How desperate did that sound?

"Brian? Are you all right? Did I catch you at a bad time?" Rush's deep voice shot through him.

All thoughts of his embarrassment faded as the blood from his head rushed south. "Just got out of the shower. I didn't hear the phone." He got control of his breathing and laughed. "I'm lying on the floor wrapped up in my sheets."

"Hot damn, darlin', I'll bet that's a glorious sight to see," Rush drawled.

"I slid across the bed to grab the phone. Guess doing that wet doesn't work."

"Let me get this straight. You're soaking wet, wrapped in sheets, and lying on the floor?"

"Yeah."

"Can you stay that way until I get there?" Rush chuckled.

"Are you serious? Are you coming to town?" Brian tried not to let his excitement show, but damned if he didn't get hard just thinking about seeing Rush.

There was a long pause, in which Brian's stomach rolled and his hopes fell. Then, Rush sighed, "There's nothing I'd like more than to see you right now, but I can't."

"Right." Brian ran his hand through his still damp hair, then he gave a nervous laugh. "You shouldn't tease me like that, get me all hard, then let me down."

"Are you hard? 'Cause, darlin', I've been hard all day thinking about you. My dick's so thick it could drive nails," Rush rumbled, and Brian's balls tightened.

Damn it, the cowboy knew he made Brian hard talking like that.

"Forget the nails. Would it drive my ass?" Brian realized he'd been stroking his cock since they started talking.

"Fuck, yeah. I'd love to drive it into your sweet hole," Rush rasped, and Brian could hear the big cowboy's breathing hitch. Brian's eyes shuttered at the thought of Rush fucking him. Of all that power, or Rush handling him, dominating his body.

"Are you naked?" Brian whispered as he lay back on the floor, shoving a pillow under his head. No sense in getting up, he could jack off right here. He reached up and pulled down the lube from his side table, then spread a generous amount on his hand.

"Yeah, naked, long, and hard. Just for you, darlin'. I'm stroking my prick, picturing you wrapped in those sheets like a present just for me to open."

"Is it your birthday?" Brian slid his slick hand over his engorged shaft, while he rubbed the head with his thumb.

"No, not until July."

"Well, it's not Christmas."

"Hell, it's got to be some holiday, somewhere."

"How would you unwrap me?" Brian squeezed the tip of his cock and a drop of precum pearled. He watched as it dripped down the side of his cock, and he let the erotic feeling wash over him.

"Hmm, now that's a poser. If I go slow, layer by layer, there's a wonderful buildup of anticipation, isn't there?"

"Yeah, slow is good." Brian slowed his stokes to match the mood.

"But if I just grab those sheets and rip them off you, that's hot, too."

"So hot, Rush, so hot." His hand pistoned, the friction of his rough hand against the tender skin of his cock was delicious.

"Which would you prefer?"

"What would you really do?" Brian prayed it was hard and rough, because that's how he'd dreamed Rush would take him.

"Fuck, darlin', I want you so bad I don't think I could wait. I'd rip those sheets off, climb on top of you and ride your ass until we both screamed."

Brian groaned, his hand working his prick like a dynamo, his eyes shutting out everything around him, until it was just him, Rush, their raspy breathing, their pumping hands, and their throbbing cocks.

"Need you, Rush. So bad," Brian moaned into the phone.

"Want you, too. It hurts, I want you so bad."

"Want to suck you. Want to suck the jism right out of your cock." Brian felt the precum build, the rising of his balls in eagerness of his coming. "Want to taste you in my mouth when you explode."

"Fuck, I can't last, just thinking of your lips on my dick, your eyes looking up at me. Here it comes, darlin'." Rush groaned. There was no mistaking that Rush had shot his load and that sent Brian over the edge.

Groaning into the phone, Brian's hot cream rhythmically splattered against his taut belly. "I'm milking the last of it, Rush, wishing you could lick me clean." He smeared his cum all over his shaft, rubbing it into the swollen head as he came down from his high.

"I'll just bet you're delicious, musky, and salty. Damn, I want you." Rush exhaled in a long sigh.

Soft, deep breathing. Brian gave a soft sigh of completion.

"This is crazy, Rush. I want to see you."

"I could come this weekend. Maybe Friday night after the ranch shuts down."

"We could hang out at my place, maybe get some dinner. That is, if we hit it off." Brian hoped he didn't sound too needy.

"Hit it off? I don't think there's any doubt about that, do you?"

"No, not really. Just giving you an out."

"You're a generous man."

Brian paused. "Are you sure you want to come?"

"I'll be there. Give me the time and directions."

Brian gave him the information.

"I'll see you then," Rush drawled, as if they'd just set up a fishing date, not to meet and make their phone fantasies come true.

"Can't wait." Brian hung up.

He untangled himself from the covers and headed back to the shower to clean up. He was so excited about seeing Rush on Friday that he had to jerk off again in the shower.

Shit. This guy had him acting like he was a horny teenager, getting hard at the drop of a dime and whacking off every chance he could get.

Friday could not get here fast enough.

Chapter Five

Brian left at seven a.m. for Austin and arrived at just after ten. After being sent from one department to another, he finally found Roberta in the archive section. Technically, he found her cubicle. It was her lunch hour, and he had to wait until she returned. He sat on the chair next to her desk and tried to keep his knee from bouncing.

At last, she appeared. Roberta Banks was a tall, middle-aged woman with a mass of dyed-blonde hair piled to dizzying heights atop her head. Being an engineer, he marveled at the construction of the permed pyramid and found it hard to drag his eyes from it. The amount of Aqua Net involved must have been near the legal limit for emissions.

Roberta cleared her throat, and brought him back to his mission. He introduced himself, and she took her seat, rolled up to her desk, and put her lunch bag away in a bottom drawer.

"Sheila called and told me you'd be coming. I must admit, you're going to have a hard time tracking this man down with only a first name."

"Well, he would have been reported as a runaway. Does that help?"

"It might, if we kept that kind of record separate from the files." She sat behind a computer terminal and began clacking on the keyboard. Like Sheila's, her nails were long but painted a deep red. Possibly another requirement with civil service, along with the long-suffering sigh.

Brian waited, this time grateful for a chair to sit on because his feet ached. He should have known that he'd have to wander the halls endlessly and should have worn his running shoes instead of his boots. Where's a hunch when he needed it?

"I'm coming up with a list of children who were pulled from the system that year. These could be kids that ran away, died, or were adopted." She tapped again on the keyboard. "I'm sorting the list by names."

Brain leaned forward and craned his neck around her monitor. A list of names appeared in a spreadsheet. "There are so many."

"This is statewide."

"He was in Houston, Harris County." Brian hadn't gotten much information from Sammi when he'd questioned him, but he did get the year he ran away and where he'd been living.

"I'll sort by the county and then delete the rest."

Brian watched as the list shrunk, but it was still long. "There must be two dozen names on that list. Are they all Sams?"

"Yes, sir. Either first, middle or last. I didn't want to take a chance and make assumptions, so I included all possibilities."

"That's a good idea. Thanks, Roberta," Brian replied. He hadn't thought that Sammi might be a middle or last name.

She sat back. "Okay, I've got a final list. Twenty-one candidates, all who fell out of the system for one reason or the other, all with Sam in their names, all living in Harris County." She hit a button and the printer next to her desk came to life.

Two sheets of white paper, holding Sammi's hopes, slid from the machine.

Brian took them from Roberta and scanned them. "What are these numbers?" He pointed to a string of numbers along the side of each name.

"That's their identification numbers. They match the case numbers. You'll have to use that to hunt down their records."

Brian glanced at his watch. The place closed at five p.m., and it was already three. "That doesn't give me much time. Where do I start?" He stood and placed the papers in his portfolio.

"Well, that was nine years ago. Sorry, but I'm afraid you'll have to start with microfiche. That's down in the basement." She gave him a rueful smile and a shrug.

"Roberta, I can't thank you enough." He passed her his business card. "If you ever need help, call me."

She stared down at the card, nodded, and then placed it in a drawer. "You're welcome, Mr. Russell. Anything for a friend of Sheila's."

Brian left, headed to the elevators and down to the basement.

* * *

All day as Rush went about his chores, he had a growing sense of uncertainty. He hadn't intended to go farther with Brian than the phone sex. Fuck, the guy turned him on like no one ever had, and sure, he wasn't getting any younger, but damn it, he was fooling himself to think he could have a life with a man.

Not around here, anyway.

As he sat on his horse, looking down from the pasture to the large white house below, he knew he would never leave the ranch. The Double T was his home, his family's homestead for over one hundred and twenty years, and he'd be damned if it went under on his watch.

Spring Lake was a small town, and Rush was sure they'd never seen a gay man, much less a gay cowboy. He'd spent the last fifteen years hiding who and what he was from everyone in Spring Lake. How would it affect his reputation and his business if he came out? Without selling his livestock, the ranch would be broke in no time.

And what about Brian? They lived worlds apart. Brian's life was in Houston, his business as an investigator, his friends, probably his family. It would be the height of arrogance to think Brian would give all that up for him. Especially when Rush knew he wouldn't give up the ranch for Brian.

No matter how bad he wanted a life with someone.

Rush clicked his tongue, and the horse started off, heading down toward the barn. The hands were finishing the work on the fence and didn't need him to oversee them.

Tonight, he'd call Brian and tell him something came up, that he couldn't make it.

Long-distance relationships never work, anyway.

Rush chewed his bottom lip. He'd never had a relationship with a man, just a series of one-night stands, mostly quick, nameless sex, and he made it a point never to hang around long enough to cuddle, much less have breakfast. He'd made a choice when he was younger, knowing his life was right here.

With Brian, he'd felt, no, he'd known, there was a man he might want to wake up to in the morning, might open up to, might let into his heart. Might change his mind about living alone.

And that terrified Rush.

* * *

"Ten minutes until closing," a woman said as she tapped Brian on the shoulder.

He sat back, stretched, and rubbed his eyes. They felt as if they'd been buried in sand and then reinserted into their sockets. Going through the microfiche on the ancient machine was going to blind him.

Checking his watch, it was almost five o'clock, and he hadn't made a dent in the list. In order to find out if the kids were even the same age as Sammi would have been required pulling up each file, putting it in the machine, and going through it to find the necessary information. So far, there had been no clear leads, but he still had the bulk of the names to go over.

He groaned, realizing he'd have to stay in Austin overnight to finish the next day. Picking up his list, he dropped the paper into his portfolio and headed to the elevators.

Sammi would just die if he knew it would take two days of his hard-earned money for Brian to check out these leads. He decided not to tell Sammi. He didn't need the money, and what Sammi didn't know wouldn't hurt him. The young man had pride, even if it was newly found. Brian could understand and respect that.

As he got into his car, he turned it on, hit the onboard navigator, and called up the nearest hotel. After scanning through the selections, he found one that was reasonable and nearby. Brian called, booked a room, and then looked for somewhere to eat.

He was starving. Missing lunch had been a bad idea. Now, he scanned the listings for the closest buffet. All he could eat sounded damn fine to him. Then, back to the hotel, get clean, and go over the list of names.

Maybe, he'd get a hunch about one of them.

Go straight to Go. Collect two hundred dollars.

Lately, his gift had been strangely silent. And that worried him.

Then, between heartbeats, between breaths, between the blink of his eyes, it came to him. Something big was coming, and he knew when it hit, if he wasn't careful, it might just knock him off his feet.

* * *

Rush stared at the phone in his hand.

More than anything, he wanted to see Brian. What was the point? He'd fall in love with Brian, they couldn't be together, and his heart would be broken. He'd avoided that fate for a long time, why let it happen now?

Best to call and break it off. End it before it went too far.

He flipped open the phone, hit his contact list, and brought up Brian's name. Biting his lip, he hesitated as his finger hovered over the pad.

Maybe he shouldn't call. Maybe he just wouldn't show up on Friday.

Coward. That was a shitty way to dump someone. Especially a man like Brian. That sort of attraction didn't come along every day, Rush realized that much. He should be open and honest about his feelings and his fears.

Open and honest were things he did not do well. What would he say? "Sorry, darlin', I'm too fucking scared of being hurt to take a chance on you? Forget it, babe, you're not worth me giving up my ranch?"

He pushed the phone against his leg and snapped it closed.

* * *

Brian stretched out on the hotel bed farthest from the air conditioner. It was chugging along, shooting tepid air into the room. All in all, it wasn't a horrible room. He'd checked the sheets and they looked clean enough.

Picking up the TV remote, he flipped through the hotel's offerings. Not much. A few ESPN channels and some pay-for-view. His eyebrows rose when he came across a porn channel. He dropped the remote on his stomach and watched.

Some porn star queen was giving head to some obscenely endowed dude. Guy was lying there, arms behind his head and eyes closed as if he was asleep. Brian snorted. Hell, woman or not, if anyone was sucking on his dick like this woman was doing to that guy, he'd at least open his eyes and fucking watch.

Frustrated, he turned it off. He didn't want to watch anyone else. He wanted Rush. Shit. Just the thought of talking dirty to Rush got him hard.

He reached for his phone, flipped it open, found Rush's name and hit send.

After a two rings, Rush answered, "Hello?"

"Rush." Brian sighed. God, his cock throbbed.

"Darlin'," Rush exhaled. "Miss you."

"Miss you. Need you, cowboy." Brian flicked open the button of his jeans, slid down the zipper and splayed his pants open. His cock bulged, trying to break through his briefs.

"Fuck, Brian, this is nuts. You get me so horny."

"My dick is weeping for you, cowboy." Brian pushed down his briefs and pulled out his cock. The leakage dribbled from its eye. He thumbed it over the head and hissed.

"I jerked off first thing this morning. Called out your name, darlin'," Rush drawled.

God, his voice sent shivers down Brian's spine. "I'm so hard for you, I'm aching."

"You know what to do."

"Yeah. Fuck, I want you to suck me. I'm getting tired of my hand."

"Me, too. My wrist and elbow are sore as hell. How am I going to explain it to the doctor? Been jerking off like a fifteen-year-old with raging hormones. Got a guy that keeps me hard all day and makes me come in my sleep. Can you do anything for me, Doc?" Rush laughed, deep and rich.

"That reminds me. Are you clean?"

"I get tested every six months. Clean as a whistle. I'm very careful," Rush assured him. "You?"

"I'm clean. I always wear a condom."

"Me, too."

"Never found the man I trusted enough to go natural with. I'm saving it, I guess." Brian gave a wry chuckle.

"For that special someone?"

"Yeah. Sounds silly, huh?" Brian wanted Rush to be his someone special, but if he mentioned the "love" word too soon, Rush would probably bolt.

"No, sounds good." Rush exhaled long and slow.

"You working it, cowboy?" Brian wanted to hear Rush talk to him.

"Using two hands, darlin'. One's squeezing my balls, the other's stroking my prick. I'm buck naked, stretched out on my bed, with a hard-on just for you."

Brian groaned. "All six foot fucking four of you? Want to lick every inch of your body. Want to suck your nipples until they're hard as bullets. Want to run my fingers through the hair around your cock. Cup your balls. Suck them." Brian panted, as his hand shot up and down, his thumb brushing over the tip, pumping as if he were going to die if he didn't explode.

"Goddamn, darlin', this is killing me. I'm so hot I'm going to blow my load. Tell me you want me," Rush begged.

"I want you. Want you to fuck me. Ride me like a fucking horse. Slam into me—"

"That's it! I'm coming. It's so fucking sweet. Brian, goddamn!" Rush cried out.

"Right behind you, babe." Brian's fist flew like a fury over the rim of his head, and his release shot through his prick, exploding onto his belly. "So good, Rush, so good." He sighed.

Hard, deep panting slowed to soft, shallow breaths.

"Fuck, we've got to stop this." Rush laughed.

"It's only going to get worse. Once I have your ass, I'm going to want you all the time," Brian confessed. "What will we do then?"

Silence.

Brian's stomach flipped. Shit.

"You there, Rush? Did I say something wrong?"

"No."

"Are you sure? You're real quiet." Brian knew not to push, but couldn't help himself.

"About seeing each other…" Rush hesitated.

"What about it? You're still coming tomorrow night, aren't you?" Brian licked his lips. His mouth had gone dry, and all the moisture in his body seemed to have dried up.

Rush inhaled over the line. His breath held for what seemed a lifetime. Brian waited for Rush to speak.

"I'll be there." Rush exhaled.

"Did you just light up?" Brian recognized the sounds of smoking.

"Yeah."

"You shouldn't, you know," he said softly.

"I know. But it's one of my few addictions."

"What other addictions do you have?" God, Brian hoped there was nothing serious. He was just straight laced enough to abhor drugs and even though he drank, there was a big difference from that and being an alcoholic.

"Well, I never met a pair of boots I didn't like."

"That's harmless enough. I feel that way about coffee mugs," Brian admitted.

"And I find it hard to resist a newborn calf or foal." His voice took on a teasing lilt. "It's those big brown eyes, surrounded by thick dark lashes, sort of like yours. They get me every time."

"Good to know. What else?"

There was a long pause and a sharp inhale. Brian held his breath, knowing something big was coming.

"You," Rush breathed. "I can't get enough of you, and it scares the crap out of me."

Chapter Six

Brian was speechless. After he swallowed and steadied his breathing, he whispered, "I know. I'm scared, too. This is really intense. Like nothing I've ever experienced."

"Yeah, that's just it. I've never wanted a man as bad as I want you."

"I'm afraid I'll screw this up, and if I do, it'll never come again." Brian opened a piece of his heart to Rush. It might have been foolish, it might have been too soon, but he couldn't help himself.

"Look, I'll be there tomorrow, but I'm not promising anything, Brian." Rush's voice turned sharp and impatient. "This is hard for me."

"I understand. Can we just try? I know we're both frightened about this, but can we at least give it a chance?"

"I'll see you then." Rush hung up, leaving Brian's question unanswered.

Brian rolled off the bed, undressed, and hit the shower. He had to get a full day's work in tomorrow and with the questions that were swimming around in his head that might just prove harder than he'd thought.

* * *

Rush woke with a world-class hard-on. Groaning, he knew it wasn't a piss erection; the ache was too primal, coming straight from his balls, not his bladder.

Fuck. Brian had him so hot and horny he couldn't stand it. And despite all his declarations of staying away, he'd agreed to go to Houston and meet Brian. Again, he ran through all the reasons he shouldn't go. There was a long list of those and only one reason to make his date.

The chance that Brian was the man he could share his life with. If he didn't go and find out, he'd call himself a pathetic coward for the rest of his life. And the Weston men had never been cowards. Not his grandfather, his father, not young Robbie. And until he'd met Brian in that alley, he hadn't thought he was either.

In truth, he was a coward. He'd been one for fifteen years, hiding what he was from the town, sneaking off to Houston for casual sex, and keeping every man he'd ever met at an emotional distance.

He reached for the lube, spread some on his hand, and tossed it down. Lying back, he closed his eyes, and Brian's face surged unbidden into his imagination.

Brian, stretched out beneath him, moaned softly, as Rush pumped into him. Eyes closed, his tongue passed over his full lips, driving Rush crazy with the desire to kiss them. Instead, he worked the long length of his dick, stroked the oil over the engorged tip, and slid his hand back down the sides of his shaft, and squeezed his balls.

He was so close to coming that it took nothing more than imagining Brian's mouth sucking in his balls, first one, then the other, the incredible tingling and sweet pain as he pulled them away from Rush's body, to send Rush over the edge.

Crying out, he emptied onto his belly, long white streams of jism splattering warm against his skin like heavy raindrops on a window. After a shudder, he fell back and tried to catch his breath.

"I swear, I'm going to have a fuckin' heart attack tonight." Rush groaned.

If he knew one thing, it was that phone sex was not enough. He wanted Brian in the sweet, delicious, mouthwatering flesh. Wanted him more than he'd ever wanted anyone else. Most of the men he'd fucked had been easy to walk away from. All of them casual, most anonymous, just used to satisfy the need for physical gratification.

Because Rush could never bring a man home to the ranch. Not while his father had lived, and not while his mother had lived. Now, both of them were dead, buried next to Robbie on the hill behind the house.

Rush slung his legs over the side of the bed and put his head in his hands.

There was no one standing in the way of his happiness.

Except himself.

Fear, like some huge wall of ice, had hardened his heart all these years. Fear of exposure, fear of his parent's disappointment and rejection, and fear of opening himself up to a man and of being hurt.

On one side stood Rush.

On the other stood Brian.

The wall separating them was immense, cold, hard as steel.

Fuck. Two big men like Brian and Rush should be able to take down that wall, shouldn't they?

* * *

Another day spent in the basement of the CPS building, spinning through miles of microfiche, Brian's eyes going crossed as he watched files blur past.

He was down to three possible candidates. The rest of the names had been crossed off the list, but these three had stayed. Now, he pulled up the first one.

A kid named Samuel James Waters. Brian pulled up his record and began going through the images of the boy's folder. The first materials were the most recent, eventually going back until the child had first come into the system.

He had attended high school on the north side of Houston until the day he didn't show up. Reported missing by his foster parents Jason and Donna Rankle, not Don and Jan Ranks. Sammi's memory was awful, but Brian supposed that to Sammi, they had been just more of the same. Sammi had been with them for only six months.

Prior to that, he'd been assigned to a group home for almost two years. That would put him at about thirteen years old. Brian scanned a notation about a fight. He stopped at another entry, read it, and groaned. A report about Sammi being raped had been filed by the social worker for the home. No charges had been brought against the alleged perp, one of the older boys, and he couldn't find any record of a follow-up investigation.

Shit. Brian couldn't imagine being raped at thirteen. No one to back him up, or to come to his defense. Nothing done about it. What a fucking nightmare.

Another form. Another set of parents. Sammi had lived with them for almost a year before they sent him back. Brian read their statement. Vague, they talked of Sammi's oddness, and their worry that he was dangerous.

Brian shook his head at the wrongness of that statement.

Sammi was many things.

Tender. Vulnerable. Sexy. Loving. Self-sacrificing.

But dangerous was the last thing he'd ever call Sammi.

Sammi had returned to a group home, this time only for a few months. A new set of parents. These lasted over a year. Sammi had been returned, yet again. Same sort of comments from the foster mom and dad.

Brian scrolled past more of the same. The pattern was clear as day. Sammi would be fostered out, the parents would return him after six months to about a year, and back he'd go to the group home. Lather. Rinse. Repeat as necessary.

When Sammi was ten years old, Brian found a report of alleged sexual abuse filed by the social worker against the foster father. Sammi had been removed from the foster home and sent back. Again. Nothing had been done about the bastard who'd abused him.

He'd thought being raped at thirteen must have been horrible. Sexually abused at ten by the person who was supposed to protect you?

That Sammi had survived, had grown into the incredible, giving person he was floored Brian. Mitchell had fallen in love with Sammi without knowing any of this crap. Did he know this stuff now? Had Sammi told him of his past, and if not, should Brian?

Knowing Mitchell, it wouldn't make a difference to him anyway.

Brian scrolled farther back into Sammi's past. More of the same. It was heartbreakingly sad.

A photograph stopped him. A dark-haired little boy stared into the camera with eyes so old, so sad, and so deep that it sucked Brian's breath from his chest. Sammi stood apart from the man and woman holding hands. A stranger in what should have been his home, among the people who were supposed to care for him. Instead, he'd been tossed back and forth as if he were a human hot potato, with no one wanting him.

Sammi's life had been a tragedy. But he'd survived, and now he flourished under Mitchell's love, his acceptance, and his belief that Sammi could be so more than what he'd been.

Leaning back, Brian closed his eyes and rubbed them. What would he have done with an odd child like Sammi? And he had to have been strange. His power to know what people were thinking and feeling must have creeped the shit out of everyone.

Had Sammi even known what he could do? How did he deal with it as a young child? Obviously, he'd managed it, but only just. If not for meeting Mitchell, Sammi would have been sold by Donovan to some bastard in Italy and sent overseas to serve whatever perverted needs his buyer might have possessed.

Brian got back to work. Only two hours before closing and the thought of coming back next week made him groan.

The blur spun, then stopped. Brian focused his eyes.

Sammi's initial papers.

With his pen poised over his pad to write down the needed info, Brian leaned in as he read the transcript of the mother's statement given when she'd abandoned her son to the state. He skipped over a long section of the social worker's questions and began to read when he reached the part about why Sammi's mother had given up her child.

Mother: *"I can't stand it anymore. Can't deal with it. You've got to take him. It's too late for me. Too late. Save Sammy."*

Social worker: *"What do you mean, too late?"*

Mother: *"No more time left. Sammy needs to be safe. From the voices. From me."*

Social worker: *"Do you want to hurt him?"*

Mother: *"No, no, no. The voices. I have to stop the voices."*

Brian sighed. Sammi's mother must have had the same power as he, only she hadn't known what it was or how to handle it. It was clear to him that she'd teetered on the edge of desperation and sanity. In her own way, she'd tried to save

Sammi from some horrible imagined fate, unaware of the true fate she'd left him to.

Well, what would Brian think if he could hear everyone around him? All their thoughts and feelings? He'd think he was fucking crazy.

Just like Sammi's mother.

The papers had been signed, notarized, and it was done. Sammi had been made a ward of the state. And his mother? No note in the file about what had happened to her.

Brian wrote down her name. Lydia Mae Waters. Finally, a last name. She had been nineteen years old, and Sammi had been only two years old, not three. Was that her married name? Chances were, at seventeen, she hadn't been married when she'd gotten pregnant. He'd have to check the records, but with a last name to work with, it should be easy.

He scrolled to the end of the file and froze.

Bingo. Sammi's birth certificate.

Samuel James Waters. Mother— Lydia Mae Waters. Father— none given. Born— March 13, 1984 at Hermann Hospital, Houston, Texas. Time— Six sixteen a.m. Weight— Six pounds three ounces. Length— Nineteen inches.

How lucky was that? Now Sammi had everything he needed to order his birth certificate online and to apply for his social security card, and with those two small pieces of paper, an entire future would open up for him.

Brian loved this part of his job. He'd actually done it, found out who Sammi was, and with this information, Sammi could have a future and a life as a "real" person, not some shadow entity operating below the radar of the "real" world.

Gathering his papers, Brian stood and switched off the machine. Two long days, but it had been worth it.

Brian thanked the woman at the desk as he left. If he hurried, he'd make it back to Houston before Rush showed up at his house. Maybe he should call, let him know he was running late, so the big cowboy wouldn't worry.

Humming, he rode the elevator to the main floor, exited the building, and headed to his car.

Tonight, he was finally going to get his hands on the cowboy of his wet dreams.

Chapter Seven

Rush felt as nervous as a fifteen-year-old on his first date. Shit, if the truth were told, it was his first date. With a man. He'd only gone to bars and hooked up. Now, he was going to Brian's house for dinner and what he'd hoped would be mind-blowing sex. He wouldn't think about having anything more with Brian than just sex. Just a glimmer of the word *relationship* made him want to pull off the highway, turn around, and head back to the ranch.

"One step at a time, cowboy," he told his reflection in the rearview mirror.

He took a deep breath and exhaled. His desire to see Brian, to hold him, to touch his body, outweighed all his niggling fears. He passed the next exit without getting off.

He could do this. He wanted to do this.

Good Lord, he needed to do this.

After his work at the ranch had been completed, he'd washed his truck, cleaned it out, and hit it with some air freshener to kill the smell of stale smoke. Then he'd showered, shaved, and stood at the closet door staring at his clothes, searching for just the right thing to wear. He'd taken his time ironing his shirt, making sure it looked cowboy crisp, and had put a sharp crease in his best black jeans. Shined his best black boots.

Now, as he passed the halfway point to Houston, his heart raced in his chest, his stomach a huge knot of anxiety. The eager anticipation of seeing Brian had him straining against the buttons of his fly.

"No turning back now, Weston," he muttered. Shit, he needed a cigarette, but he'd stashed them in the glove compartment. He'd forgone them once he'd brushed his teeth and used the mouthwash to freshen his breath. He wanted his first kiss with Brian to be one Brian would remember as delicious, hot, and sexy.

Glancing in the mirror, he checked his hair for the third time. Using his fingers, he ran them through his bangs, pushing the unruly mass of hair back from his forehead. It would have to do. He'd also left his Stetson at home. A choice he'd wasted too much time pondering over and now regretted. If he couldn't have his smokes, he wanted his hat. A cowboy without his hat was just plain naked.

He was running late and he stepped a little harder on the gas, inching his speed up, but still staying under the "safe" margin. A speeding ticket was not what he needed right now. He'd surely break out the cigarettes if that happened.

He tapped the steering wheel, and then he reached over to turn off the radio and punch up a CD. The station he'd been listening to had played a string of songs he didn't like. As far as he was concerned, some of this new country music was nothing more than pop in disguise. He liked his country music "country."

As George Strait filled the cabin, Rush relaxed into the seat, shook out his shoulders, and eased his white-knuckled grip on the wheel.

* * *

Brian pulled out his cell phone and hit Rush's number. After a few rings, it connected.

His words tumbled out before Rush could say hello. "Hey, it's Brian. Just wanted to tell you I got a late start out of Austin, and I might be just a little late getting home."

"No problem. I think I can wait for you." Rush chuckled into the phone and sent Brian's arousal into overdrive. He was already semi-hard just thinking of seeing Rush.

"I haven't changed or showered since this morning," Brian warned.

"And I spent all this time getting gussied up for you." Brian heard the teasing in Rush's voice and relaxed.

"Well, I would have liked to meet you for once without stinking."

"Should I just wait in my truck while you go in and get cleaned up?"

"I'm not sure..."

"Or maybe, I should come in and help. Get you wet, soaped up, scrubbed down. You know, squeaky clean." Rush's voice deepened, and Brian's cock stiffened.

"Goddamn, cowboy, you're killing me. My jeans are too fucking tight." Brian moaned. What was it about Rush that set Brian off? Every time they talked on the phone, it turned into phone sex.

"Mine, too. Since I got in the truck, my prick's been like a stick. Hard, stiff, and needing your lips on it."

Brian groaned and tried not to let his eyes roll back in his head. His hand dropped from the wheel and rubbed against his cock. It wasn't enough. Pushing back his seat for more room, he unbuckled his belt, popped the button, and slid down the zipper.

"Got my dick in my hand right now, cowboy."

"Fuck, darlin', I was just pulling mine out."

"Shit, what is it with us?" Brian said softly. This was nuts, jerking off while driving. He was Mr. Responsibility. Rush made him throw his caution to the wind, made him wild and reckless. Brought out the outlaw in him and in a way, he liked that.

"Just can't get enough of you, your voice. Can't wait to hold you in my arms, darlin'." Rush's husky whisper blasted through Brian's brain and made his balls ache.

He squeezed the tip of his cock. "Shit, I'm going to come all over my jeans."

"Use a napkin."

"Right." Brian fumbled around the seat and found a couple of take-out napkins.

"Darlin', I've been thinking about you all fucking day. Ever ride a horse with a hard-on?" He chuckled.

"No. What's that like?"

"Well, at first, it was a might uncomfortable. Then, I spread my legs, really settled my balls into the saddle. I dropped my hand off the pommel and rested it on my cock. Then, I let the rolling motion of the horse rub my hand up and down while I thought of you riding with me."

"Bareback?"

"Yeah, both us and the horse. I'd pull you tight against me as we rode, then slip my hand around to hold your throbbing flesh."

"It's throbbing right now, Rush. Can you fuck on a horse?"

"I'm not sure. Never tried it." He laughed, and it made Brian warm all over.

"We'd probably kill ourselves."

"Yeah. They'd find us lying on the ground, dead, with my dick in your ass and my hand on your prick." Rush's deep laugh boomed in Brian's ear, and he joined him.

After the laughter died down, Brian sighed. He was sure Rush could hear the longing in that sigh.

"Darlin', I want you so bad," the big cowboy whispered.

"Need you."

"We'd better stop before one of us has an accident," Rush suggested.

"You're right. I tend to lose control when I come."

"I'd like to see that."

"What about you? What happens when you come?"

"Fuck. Lately, I've just been calling your name."

"Oh, shit, cowboy, why'd you have to go and say that," Brian groaned.

"Can't help it. Just want you so fucking bad."

"I'm hanging up. Before we crash and burn."

"Fine. Be like that. But you better watch out when I get there," Rush's voice sounded dangerous. Brian loved it.

"What are you going to do?"

"Make you scream, darlin'. Make you scream," Rush rumbled, then hung up.

* * *

Brian turned the corner. A black Ford F-250 had parked in front of his house. His mouth went dry, and his throat closed. Wiping his sweating palms on his thighs, he took a deep breath and held it.

Rush.

His cowboy.

His cock stiffened. Ignoring it, he pulled into his driveway, parked, and got out.

The passenger door to the Ford opened, and Rush leaned toward him. In the fading light, Rush's blue eyes seemed to glow from inside the darkened cab. His hand held the steering wheel as he leaned forward, and his arm rested on the back of the bench seat. Dead fucking sexy.

"Get in, darlin'," Rush beckoned, and Brian couldn't resist.

After a quick glance around the street, Brian slid onto the leather seat and closed the door. He was here at last, sitting in Rush's truck, the scene of so many of his fantasies about his cowboy.

Just like in his very first fantasy, they stared at each other, fire burning in their eyes. Brian had thought they'd throw themselves at each other in a rush of animalistic need, but the atmosphere in the truck was different somehow.

Slower. Sexier.

Rush reached for Brian and slipped his hand around Brian's neck, his fingers burying themselves in Brian's short hair. As Rush's thumb stroked his jaw, Brian could feel the man's calloused skin as it pulled across his day's growth of beard. It was heaven and his cock begged for release.

Those blue eyes held his in a grip. Nothing existed but him and Rush, the cab of the truck and this moment. Rush pulled him forward, gentle yet firm. As Brian slid across the bench, he reached for Rush. His hand landed on Rush's thigh and curled over it. Rush's lips parted, Brian closed his eyes and they met in a tender kiss. Soft, yet firm full lips cradled his, and he sighed into them. Rush's other hand dropped from the back of the bench to join the other in cupping Brian's head and controlling the kiss.

Lingering, they parted, joined again, and deepened the kiss. Rush's tongue played across Brian's lips, his teeth gathered Brian's bottom lip and gave it a soft tug. Brian groaned and, eager for Rush's tongue, opened his mouth.

Rush entered his mouth, tongue searching. He stroked Brian's tongue, circled it, and withdrew. Rush tasted faintly of spearmint toothpaste, and just a hint of cigarette. Delicious. Brian committed the flavor to memory.

He slipped his tongue into Rush's mouth where it was captured and thoroughly sucked. Brian's balls tightened, and he knew just kissing Rush could make him come.

Not yet. Hell no. He needed so much more.

Sliding his hand up Rush's leg to his crotch, Brian avoided touching Rush's straining erection. He pulled his tongue away, and they parted. Rush sighed and rested his head against Brian's forehead.

"Darlin', darlin', darlin'," he whispered. "I've waited so long for this."

"I want it to be perfect."

"Just like your fantasy?"

"Yeah. Silly, huh?"

"No. Let's make it come true." Rush leaned back and unbuckled his belt. Brian flipped open each of the cowboy's shining metal fly buttons and pulled the jeans open. Rush's breathing was harsh, hungry, and crowded out all other sound from Brian's ears.

Rush lifted his ass off the seat as Brian pulled his jeans and briefs down to cup Rush's cock and balls, then pulled the soft cotton briefs up to showcase his package.

"Beautiful. Jesus, you're so beautiful." Brian moaned as he gazed down between Rush's muscular thighs.

Rush's long, thick cock, engorged and ready, lay against his belly. His balls, the pink skin of his sac stretched tight, were large and round and tempted Brian to taste them. Rush stroked over his prick, then slid his hand to his belly to push up his shirt.

Brian didn't know where to start.

"Your lips on my cock would be incredible, darlin'." Rush was certainly not shy about asking for what he wanted.

"Just couldn't make up my mind. They both look so fucking good." Brian took Rush's cock in his hand and pumped it. Rush groaned and laid his head back against the corner of the cabin.

Squeezing precum from the eye of the blood-infused head, Brian bent down to lick it. He swirled his tongue over the head, bathing it with the salty droplet. As he circled the rim and slipped down the shaft, Brian felt the thick veins that supplied the cock with its power to stand upright and glorious.

"Goddamn, darlin', you've got the sweetest tongue. It's so hot. I can feel your heat on my dick." Rush buried his hands in Brian's hair. "But you're killing me. I need you to take me in your mouth."

"Not yet." Brian smiled up at him.

"Shit." Rush's head fell back. "You're going to make me suffer, aren't you?"

"We'll see who screams first, cowboy."

Brian moved to Rush's balls, laving them with the moisture from his mouth until they glistened. His lips cradled the tip of his tongue as he ran them over each hard egg and then up Rush's shaft.

Rush's hips rose, reaching for another lick from Brian.

"You want more?" Brian asked, his voice husky and thick with arousal.

"Yes."

"Tell me."

"Suck me, darlin'. I need you to suck me off." He stroked Brian's head, and his fingers worked their way through his hair, as he pressed him down.

Brian sucked one ball into his mouth, and Rush cried out. Running his tongue around the choice nut, Brian loved the taste. A little salty, a little musky, all Rush. God, what would his cum taste like? He needed to know.

Moving to the other one, he gave it proper attention as Rush bucked his hips and muffled a shout. Brian pulled it, stretching the ball away from Rush's body.

"Goddamn!" Rush yelled. Brian let it go and it sprang back to nest against the cowboy's body. The sight turned Brian on and his cock jerked against his jeans.

"That was almost a scream," Brian taunted.

"Darlin', you're going to know when I scream. Promise you." Urging to him to take his prick again, Rush pushed down on Brian's head.

It was time to give Rush what he wanted. Brian wanted it also, and if he didn't move it along, he'd be coming in his jeans before he got a chance to go down on Rush.

Brian held Rush's thick member upright and swallowed it all the way down to the root until its tip hit the back of his throat.

"Goddamn! You fucking bastard," Rush cried out as Brian swallowed him. And swallowed and— oh goddamn— took him until Brian's lips touched his body. Eight fucking inches down Brian's magnificent throat. Ready to shoot, Rush's balls tightened.

Then, Brian swallowed and his throat massaged Rush's dick.

"Oh shit," he groaned. "Not yet, not yet." His head thrashed as he struggled to stop the orgasm that was building in his balls.

Brian pulled back, slipped his lips over the soft sensitive skin of his cock, and then swirled his tongue around the tip. "No, not yet."

Looking down, Rush watched as Brian glanced up at him, then hungrily took his cock again. Several deep swallows threatened Rush's resolve. He knew that when he came, it would be so good he *was* going to scream. And at this point, he didn't care if he lost the bet. He just wanted to come with Brian's lips on his dick.

Rush thrust his hips, and Brian rode him, let him pump into his mouth, so warm, so wet, his own private cavern of love. Fuck, what would Brian's ass be like surrounding his cock?

Brian had his hand wrapped around the base of his shaft. Goddamn, Rush was in heaven. Jerking him off, sucking him off, Brian brought him off like no one else ever had.

All Rush knew was that he wanted Brian.

His balls slammed into his body, and in that exquisite moment, he hung on the edge of release. "Brian, oh, darlin', I can't hold back." With a shudder that racked his entire body, it broke over him, flooding past all his defenses. His cum fired down his prick and exploded in a mind-shattering orgasm.

Rush screamed.

Brian plunged down to catch the hot load of cum that barreled out of Rush's cock and hit the back of his throat. He swallowed the delicious cream. And swallowed. And swallowed until he'd memorized the flavor and sucked Rush bone-dry.

Rush, shaking and eyes closed, fell back against the seat as he gasped for breath. Brian left his spent dick with a sweet kiss, licked his lips, and leaned in to give Rush a kiss. Their open lips met, questing tongues tasted, and then Brian pulled away.

"Made you scream, cowboy." Brian tried hard to keep the smug look from his face.

Rush opened his eyes and shook his head. In a shaky voice, he said, "Christ. You win. Uncle."

"Don't ever forget it, either. I'm the one that made you scream." Brian felt proud and possessive. This was his cowboy. Everyone else could just back off.

They locked gazes. Rush could see the all emotions Brian's dark eyes held, fought to keep the same from showing in his.

That's when Rush panicked.

How could he let this happen? As he looked at the man of his dreams, feelings he'd sworn to never have swelled inside him. Feelings he'd rather not name. Feelings he knew had no future.

This had been a bad idea. He never should have come, never should have agreed to meet Brian, and never should have left the ranch.

What he should do was leave.

"Rush?"

Rush looked into Brian's questioning eyes. What he saw in them made it impossible to swallow and his chest tight. Shit. He wasn't ready.

Not for this.

Not yet.

Maybe not ever.

He fumbled as he buttoned his fly and as he fastened his belt, anxiety and fear ripped through him, putting urgency into his movements.

"I can't stay, Brian." He looked everywhere but into Brian's beautiful brown eyes.

"What?" Brian sat back. "What are you talking about?"

"I only came for this. I have to be at the ranch early in the morning. A buyer is coming out to see some bulls." He tucked his shirt back into his jeans.

"Why didn't you say so before?" Brian tried to keep the hurt from his voice, but Rush wasn't looking at him. Brian's stomach flipped, but in a bad way.

"In the heat of the moment, it slipped my mind." Rush shrugged and put one hand on the wheel and, with the other, started the engine.

Brian looked at Rush's hand on the wheel, then up to his face. "Oh. I understand." He didn't understand at all. How could Rush forget to mention something like that? What happened to their plans? He'd thought Rush was going to at least try.

"Great. Look, I'll call you tomorrow." Brian knew a brush-off when he heard one, and this one felt as if he'd been hit in the nuts with a broom handle.

"Sure. Okay." Stunned, Brian opened the door. He hadn't seen this coming, like a car that appeared out of nowhere and T-boned him, sending him spinning.

"Sorry I can't stay." Rush smiled at him.

Brian got out and held the door open. He took what in his heart he knew to be his last look at the cowboy, then shut the door, and Rush's truck pulled away.

Rush was running.

Running back to the safety of his ranch.

And running away from Brian.

Chapter Eight

Rush made it to the highway before the shaking stopped. Acid churned in his stomach and Rush was on the verge of throwing up.

"You fucking coward!" His shout echoed in the cabin. Slamming his fist on the dashboard, he cursed and then dashed the back of his hand across his eyes.

This proved it. Of all the Weston men, he was the lone coward. Couldn't face his sexuality, couldn't face his parents, couldn't face the town.

Couldn't face the man he – shit, no. "Don't go there, Weston. Don't you dare go there," he warned his reflection in the rearview mirror.

He didn't know how anyone did it, took the plunge and just came out and said, "I'm gay. This is who I am. This is how I'm going to live my life."

The amount of courage that took boggled Rush. It was more than he had, for damn sure. Tonight just proved it. It was one thing to go into town for some action and blow off a little sexual tension, another to have a homosexual relationship.

But, sweet Jesus, he wanted Brian.

He snorted. He'd known it would come to this if he'd continued this dangerous, delicious, flirtation with the man of his dreams. Someone was going to get hurt, and tonight it had been Brian.

Everything had been so clear in Brian's face. The pain, the bewilderment. Shit. The hurt. Seeing it had made Rush feel lower than pond scum. He was a coward *and* an asshole. Great. What a combo. Hurting Brian had been the last thing he'd wanted to do, but he'd managed to do it up right.

It hit him like a fist to the gut, and his breath exploded outward. He'd never get another phone call from Brian. Never hear his deep voice, his warm laugh, his sighs of pleasure and that sweet little moan he made just after he came. Rush's stomach caved in on itself and his eyes filled to overflowing.

He'd blown his chance with Brian. Fuck. How was he ever going to— what?

Go on? Live? No, he'd get over it. He'd been alone all this time with no intentions of spending the rest of his life with someone. What had changed?

Brian. Brian had changed everything. Brian had made Rush dream of another ending to his life story. A fool's dream.

Rush jerked his chin up.

Good thing he'd ended it when he did.

But, goddamn, how sweet Brian's lips tasted. So damn good on his cock.

* * *

Brian trudged up the stairs to Mitchell's apartment and knocked on the door.

As soon as the door swung open, Brian blurted out, "I need to talk."

"Come in." Mitchell stepped aside and let him in. Brian headed straight to Mitchell's bar and poured a whiskey. With one quick toss, he downed it.

"Hell, you look like you've lost your best friend, but I'm right here, so it must be a man." Mitchell sat on the couch, waiting for him to speak.

Brian slumped into the recliner, flicked the lever, and laid back. "Yeah. It's a man." He ran his hand through his hair and then across his face.

"The cowboy?" Mitchell asked.

"I don't know what happened. We had a date. Or at least, I thought we had a date. He was supposed to come over tonight. Do dinner. Do me." Brian gave a half-hearted laugh he didn't feel. "He was waiting in his truck when I got home. Told me to get in and I did." He stopped and gathered himself. "Then, we… then I…"

"Jesus, Brian, did you do him in the truck?" Mitchell sat up.

"Yeah." Brian couldn't help but feel guilty. He'd never even had sex in a car before. He'd always considered it trashy and low class. He was better than that. Right.

"I don't *fucking* believe it. *You* had sex in a truck parked outside your house? Mr. I'm-Not-That-Kind-of-Guy? Whoa, this man must be something special for you to do that."

Grinning, Mitchell shook his head. "So what went wrong?" His eyebrow cocked up.

"I don't know." Brian shrugged. "As soon as he came, he said he couldn't stay. Started the engine and I got out. Said he'd call me later." Brian grimaced and rolled his eyes. "Shit."

"Goddamn, Brian. I'm so sorry. I know you were really looking forward to seeing him."

"Just tell me he didn't use me. Tell me I wasn't just phone sex and a hookup." Brian looked at his best friend. If anyone would tell him the truth, it would be Mitchell. It might hurt, but it would be the truth.

Mitchell shook his head. "Sounds to me like a classic 'booty call.'"

Brian groaned and put his hands over his face. "That's what I was afraid of."

Mitchell was silent. Brian knew Mitchell wouldn't give him a hard time about it. That's why he'd run straight to Mitchell. Just like always.

"I've worked so hard to not get involved in the fast life. Not to be a stereotypical queer." He spit the word out. "No bars, no nameless hookups. Just nice men in nice relationships. They may never have worked out, but they never made me feel as low and as cheap as I do right now."

"Don't blame yourself. He misled you. Plain and simple. He let you believe it was a real date. It's not your fault, Brian." Mitchell leaned over and put his hand on Brian's knee.

Brian smiled. Mitchell had always been there for him. He put his hand over Mitchell's and gave it a soft squeeze, then sat back. “Enough about my disaster of a life. Where’s the love of your life?”

“At work, but he’s getting off at eleven. I was just about to eat. Want to join me?”

“I’m not hungry, but thanks.”

“How about sit and keep me company? We haven’t just talked, me and you, in ages.” Mitchell grinned.

“Well, it’s been hard to pry you away from Sammi.”

Mitchell smiled that goofy grin, and Brian just knew he was thinking of Sammi. They were so lucky, so in love. Would it ever be that way for him?

“What can I say? Soul mates.” Mitchell shrugged and stood. “Come on. You can watch me eat. We’ll talk. I want to hear about your cowboy.”

Brian stood, followed Mitchell to the kitchen, pulled out a chair, and sat. As Mitchell puttered about, pulling out the makings for a sandwich, Brian told him about his phone calls with Rush. Sammi’s news would wait until he could tell him in person.

“So, what do you think?” Brian asked.

“Rush is scared.”

“Of me?” Brian’s brows rose.

“Of what you represent. Of commitment. A relationship, not just a casual fuck.” Mitchell finished his sandwich and took a swallow of his coffee.

“I suppose so.” Brian bit his bottom lip. “What if he calls?”

"Well, I guess you'll have to decide whether or not to speak to him, much less see him again. I can't tell you how to feel. You'll have to judge that for yourself. But I will tell you one thing."

Brian looked up into his best friend's brown eyes. "What?"

"Don't ever let anyone treat you less than you deserve. And, baby, you deserve the best." Mitchell stood, gathered his plate and cup, then leaned down and gave Brian a peck on the cheek.

"Thanks, Mitchell." He touched the spot where he'd been bussed. "So, will you marry me?"

Mitchell burst out laughing. "Now you ask! After all the times I've asked you."

"My timing sucks." Brian shrugged and laughed.

"It'll happen for you. I know it."

"Yeah? How?"

"Sammi said he felt it. That night you came over."

"What did he say?" Brian slid out of his chair and stood.

"That you're in love." Mitchell's eyes twinkled.

Brian groaned and shook his head. "Tell Sammi he's crazy."

"It's true, isn't it?"

"Even if it were, what does it matter?" He sighed. "Look, I should be going, but tell Sammi I need to talk to him."

"Did you find something?" Mitchell jumped on his words.

"That's client/PI privileged information. Strictly, need to know."

"I need to know." Mitchell cocked his head.

"Let Sammi tell you, or if Sammi wants, you can be there when I tell him."

"You're right. It's his info, his decision to tell me or not."

"See you later. And Mitchell? Thanks for being there." Brian walked to the door as Mitchell opened it.

"Are you kidding? Later," Mitchell replied.

Brian headed down the steps, climbed into his Tahoe, and drove home.

* * *

Naked, Rush lay on his bed, and watched the glowing red digits on his clock change. Two twenty-seven a.m. He hadn't been able to sleep since he'd gotten into bed. After the long drive, and what he'd been through this evening, he should have been exhausted.

He should have passed out. His body felt drained. Lifeless.

Every time he closed his eyes, he saw Brian's face and those deep brown eyes. So hurt. Rush had wanted Brian so badly, and that brief time with him had been better than any other time he'd been with a man. Ever.

Rush knew he'd made the biggest mistake of his life.

His phone lay next to the clock. In the dark, he could see its outline on the table. He picked it up, flipped it open, hit

Contacts, and scrolled three entries to Brian's. His thumb hovered over the Send button.

He should call and apologize. Explain what had happened.

He hit the button and held the phone to his ear.

* * *

Brian's phone rang. He pushed off the sofa, put down the glass of whiskey, and staggered over to the phone on the kitchen table. Leaning over, he looked at the caller ID.

Rush.

"Fuck you," he slurred.

Brian turned around and headed back to the couch. The phone's chirping pissed him off. Not that it took that much to push him. Spinning around, he snatched it up, fumbled with it, and finally got it turned off. He held the phone up and shouted, "Go to hell, you bastard." Then he put the phone back on the table and went back to the living room.

Picking up his tumbler, he downed it, then, with exaggerated care, placed it on the coaster. He lumbered off, removing his clothes on his way to his room. Once in his bedroom, he flopped face-first onto the bed and passed out.

* * *

Rush closed the phone and placed it back on the table. Pulling his pillow to him, he curled on his side and closed his eyes. Thinking of Brian, he stroked his cock, and his head reeled as blood rushed to fill his prick.

When he finally climaxed, his ragged sob echoed in the room. He rolled onto his back, limp with exhaustion and the letdown of his release, but sleep still wouldn't come to him.

He wanted Brian. But if there was one thing he knew, it was that he'd never have him.

Chapter Nine

Brian sat on a porch swing, his hand resting on Rush's thigh. Rush's arm was wrapped around his shoulder, and he was snuggled tight against the cowboy's chest. Their boots were propped up on the rail.

It felt like home.

Darkness flooded in and the scene changed.

Brian lay on his back, the hard, cold ground beneath him. Overhead, the stars flickered as clouds moved across a dark sky.

He was terrified, unable to move, frozen to the spot, and his heart beat as if it would fly right out of his chest. At the unmistakable sound of a rifle's bolt being slid back, he searched the blackness of the night.

Rush stood a few yards away with a rifle pointed down at him.

"Don't!" Brian's shout seemed to take forever coming out of his mouth, the sound of the word long and exaggerated as if time had slowed.

The flash from the muzzle was followed a nanosecond later by the crack of the shot.

Brian bolted up in bed with a shout, his arms fighting the sheets. Chest heaving, he swung his legs over the edge and cradled his head in his hands as he sucked in air.

Shit. What was that? Nightmare? Premonition?

Whatever it was, he didn't like it. It felt just like his hunches— dead certain. How the hell would they ever get to the point where Rush would try to kill him?

Launching himself off the bed, he went to the bathroom and splashed cold water on his face. As he stared into the mirror, he could see the effects of last night's drinking on his gray-tinged skin.

A moment later, his stomach rebelled and he lurched to the toilet.

* * *

Rush reined in his horse, motioned to the two hands he rode with to go on, pulled out his cell phone, and checked the time. Two p.m. He hit speed dial.

Brian's number rang. And rang. And rang.

After five rings, Rush hung up.

Brian was probably blocking his calls. And he had every right to.

He stuffed the phone back in his pocket and urged his mare to catch up with the others.

* * *

Brian stared at the name on the small display screen.

Rush. Again.

With a deep sigh, he shoved his phone back into its holder clipped to his belt. His anger of the day before had cleared like the alcohol he'd consumed to ease his pain, leaving only sadness and frustration and a hangover that was kicking his ass.

With a groan, he remembered that he should call Sammi. He needed to report what he'd learned in Austin. He searched the Contacts on his cell and hit Sammy's number.

"I have some news for you," he told Sammi after they'd said their hellos.

"Mitchell told me." He heard the excitement in Sammi's voice.

"I'd like to meet you, not do it over the phone. When are you free?"

"I'm off on Sunday. Can you come by for lunch?"

"Sure. What time?"

"About one." Sammi's breathy voice, even over the phone, was sexy. "And, Brian? Thanks."

"No thanks necessary. You're paying me to do a job, remember?" Brian chuckled.

"Right. See you tomorrow."

* * *

Another long night. Rush pulled the pillow over his head to block the sight of the clock marking off the minutes of the rest of his goddamned life. A life without love, without someone to share it with. The ups and downs, the good times, the simple pleasures.

A life without Brian.

This was stupid. He was pining over a man he'd treated no better than a cheap hookup. Not only was he a coward and an asshole, he was an idiot. He'd made the choice. He'd been the one who ran away.

Once again, no one to blame but himself.

His dad must be laughing in his grave.

He heard his old man's words as if he were right there. "There's nothing for you on the primrose path, boy. Nothing but shame." Travis Weston had stood over Rush, his fist still clenched. "I'm going to forget you ever said those words, boy. If you make me remember them again, you'll get another taste my fist and feel my boot in your ass when I kick you off my ranch."

Rush had stood, wiped the blood from his mouth, and said, "Yes, sir." He'd picked up his hat, brushed off the seat of his jeans, and climbed back on his horse.

"Thank sweet Jesus I still have Robbie." With those words, his father had mounted and galloped off, leaving Rush understanding exactly where he'd stood.

And as long as his father had lived, Rush had never again spoken of his unnatural nature nor acted on it.

* * *

"Lunch was great, Sammi. If you're not careful, Mitchell, you're going to wind up fat." Brian laughed.

"I've told him that, but he just makes me work out harder at the gym. His regimen is brutal." Mitchell shook his head but looked lovingly at Sammi sitting across the table from him.

"Admit it, Mitch. You love when I work you hard." Sammi winked. Brian knew something had passed between them because Mitchell blushed.

"Look, let's not go there," Mitchell said.

"Please. TMI, guys." Brian held up his hands. "I don't want to know. Really."

Sammi sobered and asked, "So, what is the news?" His fists clenched on the tabletop. Mitchell reached out and covered the fist with his hand. Sammi turned his hand over, and their fingers interlocked.

"First, this is your deal, Sammi. If you don't want Mitchell to hear any of this, say so now." Brian looked into Sammi's eyes almost hidden behind a long swath of black bangs.

"I wouldn't be here if it weren't for Mitchell. And you. He's been my support, and without him, I'd have never believed I could be anything more than a whore." He pulled Mitchell's hand to his lips and kissed it. "He stays."

"Good." Brian gave a short nod and a wink at Mitchell. "I found your records. Everything." He pulled a piece of folded paper from his shirt pocket and slid it across the table to Sammi.

Sammi's Adam's apple bobbed, and his eyes darted to Mitchell's.

"Go on, babe. Open it. The future awaits," Mitchell whispered and let go of Sammi's hand.

Sammi opened it, read it, and then handed it to Mitchell. “It’s all there, Mitch. Even my name.”

Mitchell scanned it and glanced up. “This is great, babe. You can get your birth certificate and social security. You’re Mr. Samuel Waters, now.”

“Can I get a credit card?” Sammi asked, tears pooling in his dark eyes.

“If you want one. But I think a bank account should come first.” Mitchell grinned.

“He just gets tired of me stashing my pay in the dresser,” Sammi shot back as he reached for a napkin to wipe the tears from his eyes.

Mitchell laughed. Sammi got up, came around the table, and threw his arms around Brian. Then he leaned down and kissed him on the cheek.

Brian felt the heat rise in his face, but he returned the hug. “I’m glad for you, Sammi.”

Sammi straightened. “Now”— he sniffed— “how much do I owe you?”

Brian pulled out another folded paper. “Here’s my bill. Ninety days, same as cash.”

Sammi opened it, read it, and then dashed off.

“Where’s he going?” Brian asked Mitchell.

“He wasn’t joking about the money in the drawer. He’s got it laid out nice and neat, as if he were a bank teller. My socks had to find a home in a basket in the closet.” Mitchell shrugged.

Sammi returned, laid two hundred-dollar bills and two twenties on the table, and said, "I hope you don't mind large bills?"

"Nope. Spends the same as small." Brian gathered the money and placed it into his wallet. "We're settled. Give me the bill, and I'll mark it paid in full."

Transaction complete, Sammi opened the refrigerator and pulled out dessert.

"Chocolate mousse."

"Don't forget the whipped cream, babe." Mitchell licked his lips as Sammi placed a tall dessert glass in front of each of their seats and added a dollop of cream on top of the rich chocolate.

"Oh, man. I can see the gym in your future, my friend." Brian picked up his spoon and dug in. "Mine, too."

Brian's phone chirped but he made no move to answer it.

"Aren't you going to get that?" Mitchell asked, pointing with his spoon at the phone clipped to Brian's belt.

"Nope. I know who it is."

"Who?" Sammi asked.

"Rush." Brian dropped his eyes to his dessert.

"Your cowboy?" Sammi sat up.

"He's not my cowboy anymore. Didn't Mitchell tell you?"

"He told me." Sammi's eyes narrowed as he stared at Brian. "He's still yours. In your heart."

Brian looked up and met Sammi's eyes. "Damn. I keep forgetting you can hear my thoughts." He shook his head.

"And your feelings. Not as clearly as I hear Mitchell, of course."

"He's right, isn't he?" Mitchell watched Brian, the look of disappointment on his face making Brian self-conscious.

"I know I should hate him for what he did. I know it. Really I do, but..." Brian shrugged and shoved another bite of mousse into his mouth.

"You want him." Sammi's simple words summed it all up for Brian.

"How long are you going to let Rush twist in the wind?" Mitchell finished his dessert, stood, and put it in the sink. He began rinsing the lunch plates and silverware and loading the dishwasher.

"Forever." Brian handed Mitchell his empty glass.

"But he's the one." Sammi frowned and reached for Brian's hand. At his touch, Brian felt a wave of hope pass through him, sent by Sammi. Damn, but Sammi had some awesome powers. They made his look small in comparison. He wouldn't mind trading for awhile. He could feel thoughts and feelings of his lover and Sammi could have the freaky hunches.

"I had a...well, I think it was a dream, but it felt just like one of my hunches. Only I've never had one come to me while I was asleep."

"That must mean it's really important." Sammi leaned his hip against the counter and stared at Brian.

"So spill it." Mitchell stopped washing dishes.

"There were two. In the first one, I was sitting on a porch swing with Rush. I think it must have been his ranch. We were just sitting. Enjoying the view. His arm was around my shoulders. I felt at peace. Like I belonged there."

"That's good," Sammi encouraged him. "Then what?"

"It all changed. It was night. I was lying on the ground somewhere. It was cold, and I was really scared, but I couldn't move. It was like I was paralyzed."

"Creepy." Mitchell grimaced.

"The creepy part was that Rush was standing there pointing a rifle at me. The rifle went off, and I woke up." He ran his hand through his hair and shrugged. "That's it."

"Goddamn, Brian. What does it mean?" Mitchell whispered.

"That Rush is going to shoot me?" Brian shrugged.

"That can't be. You love him. He loves you." Sammi shook his head, sending his bangs swinging.

"How do you know he loves me?" Brian growled. "He's never said how he feels about me, other than I turn him on."

Sammi looked at Mitchell.

"I don't care what you feel, Brian. Stay away from that fucking cowboy. You're life may depend on it. Your hunches are never wrong." Mitchell's face was fierce, and Brian's hackles rose at Mitchell's tone.

"Going to protect me? Save me from myself?" Brian's hands curled into tight fists as he faced off with his best friend.

"Well, someone has to," Mitchell replied.

“You forget I carry a gun?” Brian cocked his head to the side.

“Where was your gun in that dream? That bastard is going to try to kill you.” Mitchell glared at Brian, as angry and hard as his words.

Brian, ready to defend the man he loved, opened his mouth. All right. He’d said it, even if it had been only to himself. He did love Rush. And he couldn’t believe that Rush would ever try to kill him. Shutting his mouth, he swallowed the words he was about to say.

Sammi swooped in, wrapping his arms around his lover’s chest. “Mitch. Sweetheart. You need to let Brian handle this.” He kissed Mitchell’s throat, nipped at his ear in a blatant attempt to defuse the situation.

As Brian watched, Mitchell seemed to melt under the younger man’s kisses. Shit, if anyone was doing that to him, he’d melt, too. There was no telling what Sammi was telling Mitchell right now. Knowing the two of them and their inability to keep their hands off each other, Brian was sure it had to do with sex.

Mitchell relaxed and pulled Sammi in for a kiss. Mitchell moaned, and Sammi opened his mouth as the men deepened their kiss.

“All right. That’s it. I’m leaving.” Brian chuckled.

The lovers broke apart and grinned at him. “Sorry.” Mitchell shrugged.

“No, you’re not. I better get out of here before the clothes start coming off.” He walked to the front door, opened it, and gave the guys a loose salute. “Later.”

"Later," they called.

Just as Sammi jumped into Mitchell's arms and the two lovers slid to the floor, Brian shut the door.

His cock had hardened just watching them. Brian wanted to go home and jerk off. Shit, it was the middle of the day, and he'd planned to spend the rest of the afternoon doing yard work.

God, he missed Rush. Missed the phone calls and their incredible sex.

Mitchell might be right. But how could he be so wrong about Rush and the kind of man he was?

No. No fucking way.

Nothing would ever make him believe Rush was a danger to him.

Chapter Ten

The next week dragged by for Brian. Each day around two p.m., Rush called. On Wednesday, Brian waited in his office for the call. It was crazy, but he'd come to think of the unanswered call as sort of a love letter between them.

Rush's call told Brian, "I still care."

Brian's refusal to answer told Rush, "I'm still hurt."

His phone went off and startled him from his thoughts. It was Rush. The corners of Brian's lips turned up as he stared at the display. The phone seemed to chirp in perfect rhythm with the beating of his heart. Then, the most amazing thing happened. The message symbol popped up on the screen. Brian's heart pumped in quick time.

Rush had left a message. He'd never done that before.

Brian stared at his phone. Maybe it was important. Maybe Rush had been hurt and was lying in some hospital. Maybe he needed Brian.

Scooping up the phone, Brian brought up his messages and waited.

"Darlin'." A sigh. "I'm *so* sorry."

Brian replayed it, just to hear the cowboy's voice. Even on a message, it sent shivers of desire through him. Fuck, he was addicted to Rush's voice.

He played it again, hanging on every syllable, every nuance. Taking in that soft sigh. Was Rush smoking? Brian listened to the emphasis on the word *so*.

Carefully, he saved the message and closed the phone.

* * *

Rush pushed his hat back and turned his face up to the sun. He'd done it. He'd left a message. Once he'd decided to do it, it had taken him the better part of the day to figure out just what he would say. He'd changed it about a hundred times until he got it just right. Then he'd practiced it, mumbling it under his breath as he rode the fence. The two hired hands with him kept looking at him as if he were crazy.

They stared at him now. He didn't care. Tomorrow, he'd leave another message. He'd always hung up before it rolled to the message. Brian wasn't blocking his calls after all. He might still be hurt, but he hadn't written Rush off completely.

Maybe, just maybe, he still had a chance.

* * *

On Thursday, Rush leaned on the fence railing as three buyers looked over a selection of bred heifers. Aware that two p.m. was approaching, he fought the urge to rush them so he could make his call. Every sale was important to the ranch.

"What about those three?" one of the men asked the older buyer. Jim Bower, a longtime customer of the Double T, was shopping for a few heifers to improve his own herd and he'd brought two men, his foreman and Jim, Jr.

"I'm not sure about the one on the left," Junior put in. Rush didn't think Junior knew much about cattle from what he'd seen, but he kept his mouth shut and watched the senior Bower.

Mr. Bower squinted at the heifer in question. "She'll do, Jimmy. I'll take the three, Mr. Weston."

"Right." He called to the man inside the pen. "Manuel, cut those three out for Mr. Bower." Turning to Bower, he said, "Sir, it was a pleasure doing business with you, as always." Rush shook hands with the older gentleman, then with the son.

While Manuel separated the cattle and herded them to the chute to load into Bower's trailer, Rush walked a few yards away and pulled out his phone.

A quick push of the buttons, and Brian's number rang. Rush's heart beat like a hammer in his chest. Today, he'd leave another message, and he'd thought all morning about what it would be. He wasn't much on sweet talk, but he could at least put his feelings into a few simple words.

He listened to the message, the familiar generic female voice told him he'd reached the number and that no one was available, but since his call was important, he could leave a message after the tone. God, he wished that Brian had recorded his own message so he could hear Brian's voice whenever he needed to.

"Miss you, darlin'," Rush said and then closed his phone and put it back into the pocket of his jeans. He rejoined the group of men and watched as the cattle were loaded. Bower Sr. came over to him, shook his hand once more, and handed him a check for the cattle.

Rush folded it and put it in his shirt pocket. As Bower walked away, Rush wondered if the older man would do business with a gay man. The old man looked like he was cut from the same narrowly woven cloth as his father.

Coming out might be business suicide. It didn't make any sense to Rush.

And without someone like Brian beside him, what was the point?

Excuses. Just excuses to keep the status quo.

Nothing had changed.

He was still a coward.

* * *

Brian held the phone to his ear, closed his eyes, and listened to Rush's message.

"Miss you, darlin'."

Short and so sweet. He played it again, sighed, and then saved it.

"Miss you, too, cowboy," Brian said.

Shit. He really must be in love.

Brian grinned, then put his phone on his belt and went back to work on his computer.

* * *

Brian sat at his kitchen table eating a salad for dinner when the phone rang.

"Brian? It's Sammi."

"Hey, Sammi. How's it going?" Brian took a sip of coffee from a mug that said, "A Hard Man Is Good To Find."

"Just great. I was wondering if I could hire you again."

Brian straightened and put his mug down. "I'm here if you need me, you know that. What's the problem?"

There was a silence, and then Sammi whispered, "I want to find my family."

Brian had wondered how long Sammi would take to get to this place. He knew just knowing his name wouldn't be enough for the young man. "Well, it may take some time, but I'm sure I can locate someone." Brian didn't want to say that he thought Sammi's mother had died those years ago, and in her state of mind, it was quite probable.

"Good. Do you have enough info to get started?" Sammi's voice was a breathy whisper.

"Sammi, why are you whispering? Does Mitchell know about this?"

"Yeah. He doesn't want me to look for them. He says I'll just get hurt."

"He's probably right, Sammi. But if it's what you want, you should do it."

“Same rate as before?”

“That’s right. I can’t promise you much, Sammi. And, even if I do find your family, I’m going to have to ask them if they want to see you, you understand?”

“But, I’m hiring you.”

“Yes, but they have rights, too. And one of them is to decide whether or not they want to meet you. I’m afraid Mitchell might be right.”

“I know. He’s just trying to protect me.”

“He loves you. It’s only natural.” Brian chuckled. “And, if I remember correctly, you’re nothing but trouble.”

“That’s the story of my life.” Sammi laughed. “Okay. See what you can find and if they want to meet me. I’ll have to settle for that.”

“Good.”

“Now, when are you meeting Rush again?” Sammi asked out of nowhere, knocking Brian off-center.

“I’m not planning on meeting him.”

“Well, you should. You love him. He loves you. Just work it out.”

“Simpler said than done.” He sighed. “But, you’re right. I do love Rush. I’m just not willing to go out on a limb and get my heart stomped on. Not again.”

“Trusting is the hardest part. I should know. And if I could trust you and Mitchell, then you can trust Rush.”

“Thanks for the words of wisdom, Sammi. I’ll call you when I find out anything.”

“Okay. Bye.” Sammi hung up.

Brian finished his meal, cleaned up, and then went to his office. He brought up the folder with Sammi's name on it and went over the records he'd gathered.

The first place to start was with Sammi's mother, Lydia Mae Waters, and the first step was a quick Google search. Then, he'd move on to tracking down her birth certificate, driver's license, and, if he had to, even a death certificate.

After thirty minutes, Brian had found nothing with her name in it. It was probably as he'd suspected and she'd died shortly after giving up Sammi. But he'd need a death certificate for Sammi's closure. Until then, it was just speculation.

This would require doing research down at City Hall in the Records Division, and that would take time.

Brian pulled up his calendar and checked his schedule. The next week looked busy with two new jobs, so he might not get to Sammi until the end of the week. He opened a new appointment for next Thursday and booked the day under Sammi's new name, Sammi Waters, and then saved it.

Then, remembering how long he'd taken in Austin, he booked the following Friday.

* * *

Two p.m. Friday came and went.

Brian had pulled his phone out and checked it a dozen times. It was on, the battery was fully charged, and he had all four bars.

At three, Brian had to admit Rush wasn't going to call, and it hurt so bad it shocked him. A kick in the nuts would have felt better.

Fuck, he should have called back. He should have at least acknowledged Rush's calls. Sent him a text message, maybe. What would it have hurt to send, "Miss u 2"?

Was it too late?

He flipped open his phone and summoned Rush's number when he froze.

Sure, Rush had left messages, had called every day. But he'd never said what Brian had really wanted to hear.

Those goddamned three stupid little words.

If Rush had said them, Brian would have run to him in a New York minute. Taken him back, forgiven him all sins, and trusted him with his heart.

Rush had never said, "I love you." He'd never even said, "I care about you." Or even an insipid "I really like you."

The only thing he'd ever said was he missed him, he wanted him, he needed him, and it had all been about sex. Not love, not commitment, not forever.

Brian wasn't ready to trust his cowboy, not yet. For all he knew, Rush still thought of him as a piece of ass, a booty call. A fuck buddy.

He groaned. What a fool he'd look like, calling Rush back. It would be like begging for more, asking to be used. Like saying, "I'm a doormat. Step on me. Hard."

No fucking way. Mitchell was right. He shouldn't be treated any less than he deserved, and he deserved a lot better than Rush Weston.

Closing his phone, put it back in its holder, and decided to go to his favorite garden shop, The Arbor, and pick out some plants to add to his backyard garden. It was his favorite pastime and should take his mind off the fact that Rush hadn't called.

* * *

"Shit. Shit. Goddamn. Shit."

Rush hovered over his phone as it lay in pieces on a towel on a table in the barn. How could he have been so clumsy? He'd been mucking out the large stall he used for birthing, putting in fresh hay for the mare who was about to foal, when he realized it was just past two p.m. and he hadn't made his call to Brian.

He'd pulled out the phone to make the call, and it'd slipped out of his hand. As he'd bobbled it from hand to hand, he'd known he wasn't going to catch it. With a sickening *plop*, it'd fallen into the bucket of water he'd brought for the trough. He'd retrieved the phone, but it wouldn't turn on.

Cursing a blue streak, he'd taken it apart to dry it. But once dry, it still wasn't working.

He cursed his decision to take out the landline from the house. Without a cell phone, he was cut off. Come Monday, he'd order the landline again and put one in the barn.

He didn't even wear a watch anymore because he'd become so dependent on the damn phone to tell the time.

"Damn it." He danced around the table slapping his hat on his thigh, angry at the phone, and furious at himself.

What would Brian think?

"Fuck. Just fucking great." All his plans to win Brian back down the drain. He reassembled the phone, put his hat back on, and finished prepping the stall before moving the mare into it.

It would take him thirty minutes to drive into Spring Lake, drop by the vet's to let him know about the mare, and then go to the local phone store for a new phone.

He'd call Brian then. Leave a message. Explain everything.

In his heart, he knew a phone call just wasn't going to cut it this time.

Halfway back from town, he decided the time had come for desperate measures. Pulling over, he waited for the vehicles on the road behind him to pass, and he turned the truck around. He could be in Houston in less than two hours.

At Brian's house before seven p.m.

Chapter Eleven

Rush pulled up outside the neat bungalow and turned off the truck. Brian's SUV sat in the driveway, and the porch light was on. He was home.

So why was Rush just sitting there?

He rubbed his palms on the thighs of his jeans. Took off his hat and ran his fingers through his hair. Flipped down the visor, popped open the cover to the lighted mirror and checked his teeth. Cupped his hand and blew into it.

Stop stalling, Weston.

He'd thought about what he'd say and what he'd do when Brian opened the door. The entire drive had been a blur because he'd been so intent on what might happen.

Showtime.

He opened the door and got out, his throat tight and dry as he rehearsed the words he wanted to say.

Up the steps, onto the porch, to the door. Rush stood with his finger hovering above the doorbell. Taking a deep breath, he pushed the button. With his heart beating so hard he could feel it in his head, Rush exhaled as the door opened.

Lips parted, Brian stared at him. Rush needed those lips on him again. He cleared his throat just as Brian asked, "What are you doing here?"

"My phone got wet. It wouldn't work. I had to go to town to get a new one." Rush fumbled with his phone and held it out as if it were evidence. All the things he'd planned on saying were lost. Shit.

Brian smirked. "What? Your dog didn't eat it?"

"Dogs. I have two dogs." Rush licked his lips and gazed into Brian's deep brown eyes. Damn, but they made him forget everything except how he'd looked down into them as Brian sucked his cock.

"Two? What are their names?" Brian's smile grew.

He leaned against the doorframe as they chatted. About his fucking dogs. This is not what Rush had planned.

"Bandit and Beau." Their gazes locked. The fire between them still burned.

"What kind?"

"Huh?" He couldn't take his eyes from Brian's face. Shit, just one look at the big man and he'd gone all hard with need.

Brian's gaze slid to Rush's crotch. Fuck, Rush's jeans were straining. He couldn't take much more of this.

"Aw, shit, darlin'." He moaned, leaned forward, and kissed Brian.

For a moment, Brian melted into the kiss, and Rush's dick went rigid. He opened his mouth and ran his tongue over Brian's lips. Goddamn, he wanted inside that mouth, to taste Brian again. He'd never felt such desire for a man, and it both scared him and excited him.

Brian pushed him away. "I don't know what you think you're doing."

"Brian. Please. I'm so sorry."

"And?" Brian tilted his head to the side, waiting.

"And I want to make it up to you," Rush whispered.

"You told me you were going to at least try, Rush. Then you used me."

"I know, and I regret it. I panicked." Rush would get down on his knees and beg if Brian wanted him to. In fact, that's just where Rush wanted to be.

Brian took a deep breath, his chest swelling, and then released it. "If you ever treat me like a booty call or a cheap bar hookup again, I'm done. Understand?" The intensity of his stare did nothing to stop Rush's reaction to the man.

"I understand, and I swear that will never happen again." Rush reached out and touched Brian's cheek, cupping it with his hand.

Brian leaned into it and closed his eyes. "You hurt me, cowboy."

"Never again, darlin'," Rush whispered, leaned in for a tender kiss against Brian's full lips. They both sighed. "What now?"

"Here are the rules."

"Rules?" Rush straightened.

"You want to do this or not?" Brian growled. Rush nodded. "First rule is we go on some dates, get to know each other."

Rush had never been on a single date in his life, and the thought of being out in public with a man made his stomach do flips. But if Brian wanted this, he'd do it.

"Okay."

"Second, no leaving after sex. You spend the night or forget it."

"This goes for you, too, right?" Rush asked.

"Right."

"What else?"

"If we do this, it's exclusive, Rush. No more hookups, no more bar fucks. I want a man I can trust." Brian's eyebrows furrowed, and he looked uncertain. He didn't need to worry; Rush would give all that up. He didn't want anyone else but Brian.

"Never again. I give my word and you can take that to the grave." Rush grinned.

Brian stared at him for a moment, then continued. "Next, we keep calling during the week." Brian grinned. "I really miss our phone calls, cowboy."

"Me, too." Rush groaned and ran his hand over Brian's chest, trailing his fingers down his stomach, only stopping at the button of Brian's jeans. He flicked his fingernail against it and made a tiny *ting*. "So, are you going to invite me in?"

"No." Brian shook his head.

"What?" Rush blinked.

"Not yet. First, we're having dinner." Brian's eyebrow arched.

"Here?" Rush leaned in, his hands fingering the button of Brian's jeans.

"At a restaurant. I'm driving." He ducked back inside, grabbed his keys from a table in the hall, and stepped out, locking the door behind him.

"You're the boss, darlin'." Rush stood back as Brian walked past him. As he went down the steps, Rush admired the view. It was damn fine the way Brian's jeans snuggled his ass. Shaking his head, he followed.

After Brian pulled out of the drive and headed down the street, Rush asked, "Where are you taking me?"

"Actually, you're taking me to dinner. I'm just getting us there."

"So where am I taking you?" He chuckled.

"Just a little Italian place I know. Nice people, good food, great atmosphere."

"Sounds good. I love Italian. We only have a pizza place in Spring Lake." Rush watched Brian as he drove. The man was so incredibly handsome it took his breath away.

"Well, I hope you'll like this place." Brian placed his hand over Rush's hand as it rested on the console between them. God, it felt so good. So right. Brian's thumb rubbed over his knuckles. "Is Spring Lake very big?"

"Well, no, not really. We have all the usual fast food, but for any serious shopping or dining, you have to come to Houston."

"You live on a ranch, right?"

"Yep. The Double T."

"What's that stand for?"

"Double Trouble. My grandfather named it that after his twin sons, Travis and Trent. I suppose they were a handful." He grimaced.

"Must have been to make an impression like that. So are you trouble, like your dad?"

"What?" Rush's head snapped to look at Brian.

"You know, trouble?" Brian's voice dropped lower and he wiggled his eyebrows.

"I'm not much like my father." Rush looked out the window. He didn't want to think about his old man right now. It would bring him down off the cloud he was riding on.

Brian sobered. "Hey, if I said something wrong, I'm sorry."

"No, it's okay." Rush shrugged. He reached for his pack of smokes in his pocket and then sighed and dropped his hand to his lap. They were back in his truck.

"It's okay if you need to smoke," Brian said. "I don't mind."

"Thanks, but I don't want to mess up my minty fresh breath." He grinned.

Brian gave him a shy smile. It was so charming. "I have a confession."

"What?"

"I think it's sexy as hell." Shit. Brian's deep voice was sexy as hell.

"You do?"

"Yeah. Watching you smoke that night got me so hard I thought I was going to bust my zipper." Brian laughed.

"So smoking turns you on?"

"Only the way you do it, cowboy," Brian drawled.

Rush burst into laughter. Damn, it felt good to really laugh. Good to be sitting next to Brian, enjoying each other, and just shooting the breeze. He hadn't really talked to another man in ages, not counting talking to Manuel, telling the hands what to do, or the occasional conversation while in town or with buyers. And definitely not the pickup lines he'd used on men in bars.

The laughter died down, and they drove in a comfortable silence. Brian rubbed his thumb across Rush's hand again.

"That feels good." Rush smiled at him.

"Me, too. I like the way your skin feels under my hand."

Rush groaned. It was going to be a long night if he couldn't get his hands on Brian soon.

* * *

They'd been seated at a table for two in the half-full restaurant and had been given menus. Brian scanned his and chose the seafood Alfredo and a glass of Chianti. Rush picked the penne and shrimp in a spicy marina and a beer.

Looking over his menu, he watched Rush across the table. Shit, he was gorgeous. The candlelight bounced off his golden hair, making the highlights dance. And his eyes.

Damn, his blue eyes looked like a summer day, clear and deep blue.

Brian's cock twitched. He'd been fighting an erection ever since he'd opened the door and discovered the cowboy on his porch. Rush had been the last person he'd thought he'd find when the doorbell rang.

Thank God, Rush had come to him. And how hot had it been that Rush was so contrite, so sexy standing there, uncertain whether Brian would take him back? The big cowboy had looked so fucking cute, fumbling with his phone and babbling about his dogs, that Brian couldn't resist him.

Now, he was damned glad the red-checkered tablecloth covered his lap, and he adjusted his napkin on top of it, just in case. Brian placed his hand over Rush's.

Rush jerked it back, darting his eyes around the room.

"Fuck, Brian," he whispered. "What are you doing?"

Brian almost wanted to laugh at Rush's reaction. He had no idea Rush was so paranoid. Didn't he realize where they were?

"Rush. Chill. We're in the middle of the gay universe in Houston. Look around. Circle the wagons, cowboy, we're surrounded." Brian tilted his head toward the rest of the dining room.

Rush swept the room with a glance. His eyes widened and his hand tightened into a fist. Even though the restaurant wasn't packed, most of the tables held men. Couples. Almost all of them were holding hands, staring into their lover's faces. One pair even leaned over to steal a quick kiss.

"You know, gays don't just hang out in bars." Brian sighed. "We go to restaurants, movies, shop, and go to work, just like regular people." He couldn't believe Rush was so unexposed to gay life.

"It's not like this in Spring Lake," he said, focusing back on Brian.

"I imagine not. But the Houston gay scene isn't all bars and fucking in dark rooms, cowboy. In fact, I've never done that. I met most of my lovers in college or through friends."

Rush glanced around the room again. How could he have not noticed it? In Spring Lake, the diner was filled with men having lunch or dinner with other men, but they weren't gay, just friends or doing business.

At least he didn't think they were gay.

He chuckled at the thought of a secret underground gay brotherhood in Spring Lake. How could he get an invitation to join?

"What's so funny?" Brian asked. This time, Rush let Brian's hand rest on top of his and let himself enjoy the weight of it.

"I was just thinking that this looks the same as the lunch crowd at the diner in my town. Only the men there aren't gay. Then I thought, maybe they are."

Brian laughed. "Talk about your Twilight Zone."

Rush took a sip of his beer and nearly choked at the joke.

Over the candle on their table, its flickering light illuminating their faces, the two men gazed at each other.

"Want you, darlin'," Rush said. He wove his fingers between Brian's.

"Want you, too, but dinner and conversation first. Then I have something special planned." Brian grinned as he sipped his wine.

The waiter arrived with their meal, but Brian didn't let go. And the waiter didn't say a thing or look at them funny. Shit. If he could live his life here, with Brian, it would be a dream come true.

But he'd never leave the ranch, so there was no sense in dreaming.

Chapter Twelve

Having dinner with Brian had been more enjoyable than Rush had imagined. Brian had been charming, sexy, and funny. Rush hadn't expected funny, but he'd laughed more during the meal than he had in months. Maybe years. He couldn't help it; the enthusiastic attitude Brian carried inside about life, love, and the world around him had been contagious. Whatever Brian had, Rush wanted it.

Each time he'd been with Brian, he could almost see it. A future with a man. A life spent loving and being loved by this remarkable man. When Rush had told a few stories about the ranch, Brian had hung on his every word, as if he'd needed Rush's voice like he needed his next breath.

He'd really listened to Rush, and that was something no one had ever done. Still, their talk hadn't been serious. Rush hadn't told Brian about his father, or his brother, Robbie, or about his special abilities. Would he ever be that close to someone to share everything that he held locked up inside?

If he'd thought he was scared before, the thought of telling Brian all his secrets really terrified him. What if Brian rejected him? Thought he was some sort of freak of nature? He had to push those thoughts out of his mind and concentrate on the moment, the here and now, that he shared with Brian.

When the check came, Rush had reached for it, expecting the usual argument about who was going to pay, but Brian let him take the check without as much as a blink. And that had made Rush feel great, like he was, shit, like he was the guy.

Not to mention those killer looks Brian had given him all through dinner. The ones that said, "Oh yeah, I'm going to eat you up, swallow you down, and make you scream. Again." Have mercy, he wanted Brian to make him scream.

He'd spent the entire dinner with a hard-on straining against his jeans, hidden under the table. Now, as they drove back to Brian's, he could barely control himself.

Fingers entwined, Brian held Rush's hand.

Rush never thought just holding a man's hand would be such a turn-on, but it was the way Brian did it. His fingers would tighten and then relax, giving Rush's fingers a gentle massage as Brian's thumb rubbed lazily over his skin, sending shivers up and down Rush's spine. And every now and then, Brian would bring Rush's hand to his lips and kiss it, or give his knuckles a playful nip.

He wanted to nip Brian. All over. Small, sharp love bites. Big red love bites that would leave Brian begging to be fucked. Just the thought of having Brian's body all to himself was enough to make him fight shooting his load.

They pulled into Brian's drive and parked. Brian switched off the engine and put his hand on the door to open it.

"Wait." If Rush didn't kiss Brian right now, he'd explode. Reaching for Brian, he hooked his hand around Brian's neck and pulled him close. Their faces inches apart, Rush sighed.

Brian closed the distance, and their lips met in a tender touch. Rush felt the soft lick of Brian's tongue against his bottom lip. He moaned and opened his mouth, letting Brian in. That slick, soft, hot tongue explored Rush's mouth, felt along the edge of his teeth, and when Brian licked the roof of Rush's mouth, Rush couldn't hold back the groan.

With Brian's answering moan, Rush almost lost it. The man's throaty sound reverberated in Rush's chest as he swallowed it down, and it shot straight to his balls.

"Need you so bad, darlin'." Rush ran his hand over the hard lump in Brian's jeans.

"Not yet." Brian opened the door and slid out. "Come on." A wicked grin and a wink had Rush fumbling for the door and falling out of the cab. With a grunt, he shut the door and followed Brian as he walked down the drive toward the backyard.

"Wait." Rush halted. "I need my smokes." He trotted over to his truck, hit the remote, and opened the door. Leaning in, he rifled through the glove compartment, found his pack and lighter, and shoved them in the pocket of his shirt. Then he returned to Brian's side.

"Where are we going?" Rush didn't know why he whispered, but the situation seemed to call for it. It felt as if they were kids, sneaking down the driveway, about to do something naughty and afraid they'd get caught. Excitement rippled through him.

Holding open the gate in the tall wooden fence, Brian let Rush in, then closed it behind them. A short alley led to the backyard. The moon was a half-circle in the night sky, and Rush automatically switched to night vision. As he looked around, Brian stepped onto a brick patio surrounded by a low wall made of stones. He leaned over, and lights in the landscape came on, illuminating the trees that bordered the small patio, but the rest of the yard was in deep shadow.

Rush didn't need the lights— he could see everything clearly— but the effect was beautiful. Small floodlights cast beams of light upward into the crepe myrtles, their long trunks naked until they almost reached the top of the fence, then an explosion of green growth that blocked the view of the surrounding neighbors. Beneath them, lush hostas and ferns filled in the space. Camellia bushes filled the corners of the yard. When they bloomed, it would smell wonderful.

"Incredible." Rush couldn't think of a better word. "It's like an oasis."

"Thanks." Brian grinned at him, a touch of pink tipping his ears. God, it was so hot to know Brian blushed from his praise.

"Did you do this yourself?" Rush stepped off the patio and onto a perfect square of green lawn. "It's amazing."

"Yeah. Glad you like it. It's a work in progress. I did the patio two years ago and last year did the beds." Brian's quick smile was just a flash of white teeth and a snap of chocolate brown eyes. "Wait here. I'll be right back." He turned and went up the steps to the back door, unlocked it, and slipped inside, leaving Rush alone.

He sat on the wall and looked up at the sky. A few stars shone, far less than he would see at the ranch but, in the city, they were lucky they saw any stars at all. A few minutes later, Brian returned carrying a basket and a blanket under his arm.

"What have you got?" Rush stood.

"Just some things we might need. Here, help me spread the blanket." Brian handed it to him, then put down the basket. Rush glanced into it. There were two bottles of beer sitting in a container of ice, a box of condoms, and the lube.

Have mercy.

They spread the blanket and sat next to each other. Brian pulled off his boots and placed them at the edge of the blanket stuffing the socks inside. Rush followed his lead and placed his scuffed work boots next to Brian's brown Ropers. One of his fell over on its side. Brian's boots were smaller than his size 14s, but still at least a size 12.

"They look good together," Brian said. "Like us."

"You think we look good together?" Rush crawled over to where Brian sat, pulled him back against his chest, and stretched out his legs, bracketing Brian's. "I think we feel good together." His hands ran down Brian's arms, his fingertips tracing Brian's fingers.

"That, too." Brian leaned back, his soft *hmmm* told Rush that he enjoyed being touched.

Rush nuzzled Brian's neck, then licked his ear. "I want to feel all of you. Every inch."

"With your tongue, I hope."

"My tongue, my hands, my cock," Rush whispered into his ear. With a sharp nip, he took Brian's earlobe in his mouth. "Damn, darlin', you taste so good." His tongue traced the curls of Brian's ear, swirling tighter and tighter until he reached the hole. "I want to do this to your ass."

"With your tongue, I hope," Brian repeated and gave a soft chuckle. "I like your tongue, in case you didn't notice."

Rush laid soft kisses down Brian's neck as he unbuttoned Brian's shirt. He slipped the shirt down, feeling the hard muscles in Brian's arms as he went. The shirt landed next to the boots.

A broad, bare back rubbed against his chest, and his nipples became sharp points of need. His arms slid back up to grasp Brian by his upper arms and lowered his head to taste Brian's shoulder.

"Damn, you skin is so soft, so delicious. I love the way you smell, Brian."

Brian let out a loud sigh and snuggled against him. "I can feel your nipples through your shirt, cowboy. They're like small, hard bullets. Something getting you hot?"

"You, darlin'." He wanted Brian in the moonlight, on this blanket. "Do you bring all your men here?"

Brian stiffened, and he pulled away. "No, Rush, I don't. No one has ever been here." He twisted around to look into Rush's eyes. "I haven't brought anyone home in a very long time." Rush could see the hurt in them.

"I'm sorry. I didn't mean anything. It's just such a beautiful place, I figured… aw hell, I don't know what I figured." Rush grimaced. He'd fucked it up. He'd ruined their moment in the moonlight. Brian had probably been planning it all evening. Shit.

Brian's hand cupped his chin. "It's okay. I've never had anyone here before, but I've fantasized about it enough." A sly smile lifted the corner of his mouth.

"Fantasy, huh? Tell me." He loved it when Brian talked dirty. It made him crazy hard.

"It's just like this. We're under the stars, the night inky, but in my fantasy the flowers are blooming and we can smell them." Brian gazed into Rush's eyes.

"Who's sharing this blanket with you?"

"Different men." Brian shrugged.

"Do you know them?"

"Sometimes. Lately, it's just been you." He gave Rush a soft kiss, his lips brushing, lingering and then retreating.

"And before? Was it that friend of yours, Mitchell?" When Brian had told more than one story about his best friend Mitchell at dinner, Rush had felt of stab of jealousy. It was stupid, but he couldn't help it.

"Mitchell and I are best friends, nothing more," Brian answered quickly. "We decided a long time ago that sex would just ruin our friendship."

Maybe Brian could just be friends, but no way could Rush be friends with a man he found sexy enough to have fantasies about.

"But you think about him, don't you?" Rush whispered.

Brian swallowed, his eyes locked with Rush's. Rush could hear Brian's breathing deepen, his voice go all raspy with arousal. "Yeah."

"What happens?" Rush licked Brian's neck right below his ear.

Silence. Brian licked his lips. "At first, we're just lying here, talking, laughing. Then, Mitchell rolls over to me and begins to touch me."

"Like this?" Rush ran his fingers over Brian's chest in a caress, just skimming Brian's heated skin.

"Softer." Rush lightened his pressure. "Yeah, like that. Almost just a brushing glance. Teasing me. He doesn't say a word, just leans over, and kisses my chest. And all the time, he's looking into my eyes. Then he licks my nipples and makes his slow way south."

"Does that get you hard?"

"Yeah, makes me stiff and wanting it."

"What do you want?" Rush's warm breath tickled Brian's ear. Fuck, his cock was going to burst through his zipper.

"His mouth on my dick." Brian gasped. "I want him to suck me, lick my balls, make me come." Rush's dick jerked as Brian's hand rubbed across the front of his own jeans.

"But he's your best friend."

"Yeah. Sex fucks up friendships." Brian let out a loud sigh and let his hand drop.

"Can you be friends with your sex partner?"

"That's the ideal. Your lover *is* your best friend."

"But not for you and Mitchell?" If there was something going on between them, or if Brian held some unrequited love for Mitchell, Rush wanted to know so he could figure out a way to end it. He wanted Brian all to himself.

"No. It's not right for us. I value his friendship too much to take a chance on destroying it." Brian shook his head. "Besides, he's in love with Sammi, his life partner." Relief washed over Rush.

"Is it right for us?" Rush pushed Brian to the ground and leaned over, pressing against him.

"Want to be my best friend?" Brian grinned and looked up into his eyes.

"I want to be your best friend, your lover, your everything." Rush sighed. "I just don't know how, darlin'."

"This is a good start, cowboy." Brian pulled him down into a hard kiss.

What was his cowboy telling him? And why did Brian reveal his deepest, darkest fantasy about Mitchell? Sure, it was hot as hell and his prick had certainly responded to it, but admitting it might have been too much.

His brain had short-circuited and left him a quivering mound of want. All he knew was that he wanted Rush right now and that their lips were a perfect fit. He moaned as he arched up into Rush's body. The weight of the big cowboy felt so right. Heavy, but not smothering. The smell of him shot to Brian's balls. Leather, jeans and some musky aftershave that was familiar, but he couldn't place. Hell, was it English Leather?

The night sky, the stars, the moon, the outlines of the trees against the darkness above them all blended together to make Brian feel as if he were a little drunk, a little out of control, and a little wild.

"I need you to fuck me, cowboy." Brian squeezed Rush's ass and pulled him closer.

Rush groaned and buried his questing tongue in Brian's mouth. "Fuck, yeah."

"Take your jeans off." Brian pushed Rush away. Rush rolled to the side as the two men stripped.

Naked, they came together. Two perfect specimens of manhood entangled.

Hard shafts pressed against ripped bellies.

Brian knew no one could see them, but he couldn't care less if they did. The small chance they could be caught excited him. He'd never fucked outdoors and it'd been a fantasy of his since he'd begun putting his backyard oasis together.

Rush's hands roved over his torso, his lips pressed down on his mouth, his tongue begged to be let inside. The feel of Rush's hard length, soft as velvet, pressed against his belly, drove Brian wild.

He spread his legs, and Rush came up on his knees between them. Sitting back, he stared down at Brian as he stroked Brian's thigh.

"You're so fucking beautiful, darlin'."

Brian laughed. "It's so dark; how can you see anything? All I see is your silhouette against the sky."

Rush's head jerked up, and he sucked in air. "I don't have to see. I remember." His hand ran down Brian's thigh to his knee, then back up, circling his fingers around the edges of Brian's neatly trimmed pubes. "Did you do this for me?"

He swirled a finger in the nest, and the short hairs curled around it.

"Yeah. Like it?" Brian reached down, took his prick in his hand, and gave it a stroke. Rush's eyes widened, and for a split second, Brian could have sworn they looked almost catlike as the light from the moon hit them. Then Rush blinked, and the illusion was gone.

"Love it. I fucked a guy who'd waxed it all off once. Made eating him a delight."

Brian grimaced. "Rush, I don't want to hear about your fuck buddies or your one night stands." His body tensed beneath Rush.

Rush had screwed up again. Shit. Why couldn't he just think for once before he opened his big mouth and put both feet in? He sucked at all this sweet talk. He hadn't needed it to pick up guys in bars, just a "let's go" worked most of the time. Eventually, Brian would stop forgiving him and then where would he be?

"Want me to tell you how much *you* turn me on?" he purred.

"Yeah, that's I want to hear. Every graphic detail," Brian growled.

"I love watching you touch yourself." Rush took his own dick in his hand, and together, they pumped a long and lazy rhythm.

Brian, stretched out on the blanket, and Rush, kneeling between Brian's legs, watched each other's hands and cocks do a two-step, separate yet keeping time. Rush's panting and Brian's soft moans filled the night air of the small yard.

"Fuck, I need to taste you." Rush groaned and leaned down. Brian held his cock steady as Rush descended, mouth open, and devoured it.

Rush's lips and nose nuzzled the hair at the base of his prick. Brian whimpered.

Rush's tongue danced around the shaft. Brian gasped.

Rush's teeth grazed their way over Brian's engorged flesh as he pulled back.

"Goddamn!" Brian's shout broke the silence of the night and he sucked in air as if he could pull the word back inside his lips.

Rush smiled around Brian's dick.

"Are you trying to kill me?" Brian hissed, his hips coming off the ground in a move that pushed his cock back down Rush's throat. His hands reached for Rush's head as he buried his fingers in that tawny mane. Like some animal pelt, it was thick, rich, luxurious, and he wanted to bury his face in it, inhale its scent, feel Rush rub it over his body.

"Yeah, darlin'. Die for me. The sweet death, right?" He kissed the tip and then swirled his tongue around the fat head, catching pearls of precum. "You're so fucking plump, so juicy, so delicious."

"You'll get juicy when I shoot my load down your throat," Brian growled.

Rush didn't answer, just went down again on Brian's cock, sucking, licking, taking it all in, then pulling back. Down again.

"Fucking sweet, cowboy. Do it. Suck me," Brian whispered. He couldn't hold back much longer. Already, the sensations had built to a crescendo; his balls ached and tightened, threatening his reason. His hips rolled as he fucked Rush's mouth.

With hands splayed across Brian's belly, Rush held onto Brian's hips and took him deep. Each thrust deeper than the last. When the tip of Brian's cock reached so deep that he felt Rush choke, he lost it.

"Take it, baby, take it." Brian exploded, biting his lip to keep his scream from waking the neighborhood.

Hot, creamy ribbons of cum washed down Rush's throat with each shot from Brian's cock. So fucking delicious, he knew he'd never get enough of this man. He swallowed the last of it and pulled away, licking his lips. His hand took over, gently working Brian's cock, bringing him down from what looked and felt like a fantastic orgasm, if Brian's blissed-out expression and the shudder of his entire body were any indicators.

"Made you scream," Rush whispered. He let go of Brian's cock and stretched out beside him.

"Technically, that wasn't a scream."

"The fuck it wasn't, darlin'. It was a wonder the dogs didn't start barking and howling at the moon." Rush laughed.

"Okay. Uncle. I give in," Brian looked into his eyes, reached out and pulled Rush's hand back to gather his limp flesh. "Hold me," Brian whispered.

Rush shifted his hand to encompass Brian's heated balls, cupping them, and he felt the final shudder pass through

Brian. He leaned in and kissed Brian's lips as Brian pulled him close to rest his head on Rush's chest.

Naked, they stretched out over the blanket, wrapped in each other's arms.

"Fuck, I need a smoke," Rush muttered.

Brian laughed and pulled the blanket over them, wrapping the lovers in a cocoon of their body heat and the raw smell of sex.

Chapter Thirteen

"So, how was your fantasy?" Rush asked as he gazed up at the night sky. They'd lain silent for a long time, just being together.

Brian rolled his eyes. "Not quite complete."

"There's more?" Rush's eyebrow cocked upward.

"Oh, yeah. There's so much more." His hand slid down Rush's body, caressing, firm and smooth, until he found Rush's still engorged cock. "Like this."

Rush moaned. "Fuck, that's good." Like a cat, he stretched as he enjoyed the warmth and steadiness of Brian's hand on his heated, throbbing flesh. Watching Brian had been such a delight, but now, he meant to fuck his ass, and that would be heaven.

"Roll over," Rush commanded. Brian complied.

"Are you going to fuck me?" he asked over his shoulder, a wicked grin on his lips.

"Hell, yeah." He ran his fingertips over the globes of Brian's ass. With his night vision, he could see clearly, the lighter skin on Brian's ass, the faded tan line on his thighs from his swim trunks, the dark valley that lead to the gate to

his cum filled balls against Brian's body, and it was too goddamn much.

"Oh God, darlin'. I…I…" He couldn't say the words. He kissed Brian's cheek, licked his way to Brian's ear, and took it between his teeth and bit down.

Brian groaned and pushed back into Rush's hips as they rutted.

"You don't have to say it. Not until you're ready, love." Brian's hot breath warmed his face.

Rush buried his face in Brian's neck, lost in their primal mating. He clung tighter as his balls prepared to unload.

"Love you, cowboy," Brian whispered.

Rush sobbed once as he came, then bit Brian's shoulder to stop the string of sobs that welled from inside him as his emotional walls collapsed. He'd never heard those words from anyone other than his mother. Unaware of how much he'd secretly craved them and how long he'd denied needing to hear them, the words hit him like an epiphany, and he was struck dumb.

"Shhh…shhh…cowboy. It's okay," Brian soothed as he lay beneath Rush. Their bodies rocked, slowed, then stopped. Reaching out, he entwined his fingers with Rush's and pulled them to his lips.

Unable to think, or feel anything but a welcome numbness that stole over his body, Rush pushed off, his softening cock slipping wetly from Brian's chute. Brian rolled onto his side and gathered Rush to him with one hand and with the other, pulled the cover over them.

Back in their cocoon, warm, sated, exhausted, the lovers slept.

* * *

Rush woke, ran a hand over his face, and forced open his eyes. Dawn was creeping up on them, the grass covered in dew. He turned his head and looked at Brian, asleep next to him. Rush had never spent the night in a lover's arms, had never woken in the morning and shared the hundred little things men do to start their day.

Doing that would be the hardest thing he'd ever done.

He loved Brian. He'd known that deep inside, he just wouldn't let the knowledge become reality. Until last night. That had been a mistake.

Brian had told him that he loved him. That had been one glorious moment.

But still a mistake. Now both their hearts would be broken.

In the light of the new calm, sex-free day, Rush knew this was never going to be. In the heat of passion, he'd thought he could give up the ranch, give up his life and his legacy, but that had been just the sex talking.

His need to run slammed into him. Heart beating wildly, throat tight, he slipped from under the blanket, gathered his clothes from the pile and dressed without a sound, then shoved on his boots. As he stepped onto the patio, he paused, his back to Brian.

If he crossed the stones to the back gate, he'd be through it and out of Brian's life.

Brian had set the rules and Rush had no doubt that Brian had meant every word.

"Leaving so soon?" Brian's voice was clear, not too loud. Not accusing, either. He just sounded interested, as if he'd asked if Rush took sugar with his coffee.

"Needed a smoke." Rush reached for the pack in his shirt, dug his lighter out, and stuck a cigarette between his lips, still not facing Brian. If he looked into Brian's eyes, he'd break. Shatter into a million pieces.

"And you had to get dressed for that?"

Brian looked at his cowboy. Shoulders hunched, spine stiff, head down, the cigarette dangling from those full lips. He could only see part of the big man's face. Rush had turned away as if to shield himself from Brian.

Couldn't face him, huh? He'd been sneaking out, no doubt about that.

Brian sighed. Rush looked like a deer, unsure whether to bolt or hunker down in its hiding place. If he moved suddenly, what would Rush do?

Bolt.

If Brian knew one thing, it was that the cowboy was scared. The first time Brian had been told "I love you" had been frightening, but wonderful, and he'd walked around for weeks with a goofy grin.

Rush was frightened, all right. But there was no goofy grin, and it hurt Brian's heart to know it hadn't been wonderful, for whatever fucked-up reason Rush had.

Fucked up.

That was just what this was.

Brian pulled on his jeans as Rush smoked, one hand stuffed into the pocket of his jeans. Tense. Mute. Ready to run.

Picking up his shirt and boots, Brian walked past Rush to the back door and climbed the steps. He turned to look at the man he'd told "I love you" last night.

Rush glanced away.

"I'm fixing breakfast. Why don't you eat something before you go home?" Then he slipped inside the house, leaving the door open.

He placed his boots in the laundry room and tossed his shirt in the hamper. Bare-chested and barefoot, he prepared the coffeemaker, pulled out the bacon and eggs, and turned on the stove. Set the table.

Rush would come in or leave. That simple.

It had been too much, telling him. Still, he'd been sure the cowboy was on the verge of saying it himself. Too much, too soon. Shit. He'd ruined whatever chance he'd had with the cowboy.

He fried the bacon. Wondered if Rush liked it crispy.

Still no Rush.

Brian bit his lip as his shoulders sagged.

It could have been so good.

Rush's gaze slid to the door. He could smell the bacon cooking and his stomach rumbled. Pulling the last draw from his cigarette, he dropped it, ground it out with the toe of his boot, and blew out a stream of gray smoke. He stooped, picked it up, and looked around for somewhere to throw it.

The garbage can would be inside.

Brian was inside, cooking breakfast. Was he that sure Rush would come in?

Now or never. Cowardly cur or brave man?

It might work. Maybe they could make it work.

He'd never know if he didn't try. It was already too late for his heart. If he left, it would be broken, but if he stayed?

Rush shoved the crushed butt into the pocket of his jeans, went up the steps, and opened the door.

Brian stood at the stove.

"How do you want your eggs?" he asked, as if this was a just a regular morning and Rush hadn't almost walked out on him.

"Over easy." Rush looked at the table. It had been set for two.

"Potatoes or grits?"

"Grits." He barely got the word out.

"Coffee is almost ready. Help yourself."

Without thinking, Rush came up behind Brian, wrapped his arms around him, buried his face in Brian's neck, and inhaled. He could still smell their lovemaking, like cologne, on Brian's skin.

"I meant to the coffee, cowboy." Brian chuckled. His free hand rested on Rush's arm.

"Thanks," Rush whispered.

"For what?"

"Setting a place for me." Rush's eyes stung, and he blinked hard.

"Anytime, cowboy. Now, if you'll pour the coffee, I'll finish the eggs. Biscuits are almost done."

Rush released Brian. "Cups?"

Brian pointed to a cabinet. Rush opened it, took one look at the line of mugs, each one with a different logo or saying printed on them, and laughed. "You weren't kidding about your love of coffee mugs. Which one?"

"Guess?"

Rush picked up a mug. "Cowboy Butts Make Me Nuts?"

"That would be the one."

"I'll take the one that says, 'Where'S The Light In This Fucking Closet?'"

Brian snorted and handed him a plate of bacon.

"Crispy. Just like I like it. How'd you know?"

"Isn't that how all cowboys like it?" Brian shrugged and put the biscuits on the table.

Rush poured the coffee and put the mugs out. Brian filled the plates with eggs, spooned out some grits, and they sat.

"So, what's going on today, back at the ranch?" Brian bit into a jam covered biscuit.

"The hands are off on the weekends. I usually keep the place going, do the chores."

"Chores? Like milk the cows? Gather the eggs? Feed the chickens?" Brian's eyes twinkled and Rush knew he was being teased.

"It's a ranch, not a farm," Rush growled and rolled his eyes. "City boys."

"Sorry." Brian winced. "Bust broncos? Ride bulls? Rope doggies?"

"Something like that." Rush grinned. Brian's kidding felt natural. "More like shoveling manure, giving the horses their feed, spreading hay for the cattle. Mostly maintenance stuff. The real hard work is done Monday through Friday by my hands."

"How many do you have?" Brian asked as he buttered another biscuit. "And don't say two," he warned.

"Right now, five. But in the spring, I usually hire on a couple extra to help with the new calves."

They finished eating, and Brian gathered their plates. Wiping his hands on a towel, he leaned back against the counter. "So, I guess you best be moseying along."

"Yeah. I need to get back." An hour ago, Rush had wanted to run as far from this man as he could get. Now he found it hard to bring himself to leave.

Brian led the way to the front door, Rush on his heels. Brian reached for the knob, but Rush took his arm and pulled him back. Pressed him against the wall. Brian's hands wove into Rush's hair, their lips joined in a hungry kiss, and then Brian broke the kiss.

"Going to miss you, cowboy."

"Can I call you?" Rush leaned his forehead against Brian's.

"Anytime, day or night. I'll be waiting, dick in hand."

Rush groaned. "Why'd you have to say that? You know how talking dirty gets me hot."

Brian laughed, gave him a soft kiss, and opened the door. "If you don't leave now, I'm going to show you how a city boy uses his silk neckties to hog-tie a country boy."

Rush had to be pushed out the door. As he got in his truck, he gave Brian a quick wave goodbye.

Brian leaned in the doorway, folded his arms across his chest, and, looking sexy as hell, waved back.

A huge, goofy grin broke out across Rush's face as he drove off.

Chapter Fourteen

Brian's first job Monday morning was to go through the Houston phone book and look for Sammi's mother's name. With over four million people in the greater Houston area, the white pages were in two books, but he only had to look in the one from M to Z.

No Lydia Mae Waters. No reference to her on the Internet.

He sat back. Next, he'd look for her family, but he needed Lydia's birth certificate to find the names of her parents. That meant a trip to Houston's city hall.

He locked up the house, got in the SUV, and headed downtown.

After pulling into a nearby parking lot, Brian made his way to the building. He dumped his keys and BlackBerry into the tray and stepped through the metal detectors that guarded the entrances. Gathering up his belongings, he gave the guard a nod and headed to the elevators and the records department.

The line wasn't too bad, by Houston standards. He realized this would be a big waste of time if she'd been born outside of Houston. A dozen smaller towns were circled and embedded inside Houston; all had been gobbled up by the greedy fingers of the ever-expanding metropolis. The idea of going to each of them sucked, but if that was what he had to do to get the job done, he'd do it.

Most PI work was legwork. Boring, routine, and a huge waste of time, but absolutely necessary to doing a thorough job.

An hour later, Brian's number was called and he stepped up to the window. He presented his PI license, gave the overworked woman a smile, and asked to see Lydia Mae Water's birth record. She gave him a yellow form, and he took it down the hall to another room with another window.

The woman there, a younger version of the woman at the last window, gave him a quick check over, then disappeared to pull the records.

Fifteen minutes later, she returned and handed him a huge book. He took it to an empty spot at a table and sat down to go through it. Birth records from the year she'd been born filled the musty-smelling and yellowed pages.

Flipping to the month, he skimmed the names, turning page after page. A lot of people had been born in Houston every month, even back in the sixties. Brian sat back, stretched, and rubbed his eyes. He'd need glasses after this. Then he got back to work.

"Bingo," he muttered. His finger underlined Lydia's name. He pulled out his Blackberry and quickly entered the information. Mother's name, Rose Mae, father's name, Walter Samuel Waters. So that's where Sammi got his name. Brian included their birthdates, just to be complete, and then closed the book and returned it to the woman.

She gave him a smile that he returned, and then he left the office. It was past time for lunch, and his stomach growled. He stopped at a Greek restaurant on Montrose, had a gyros and a beer, then headed home. Tomorrow, he'd do his calling after he entered all the info into the meticulous files of all his jobs he kept on his computer.

He spent the rest of the day returning calls, talking to several new clients and turning down a job as a bodyguard. He'd done that work before, but only when his regular work was slow. Right now, business was booming. His reputation for fairness, reasonable prices, and good work was getting around.

If this kept up, he might have to hire someone to help him.

He grinned and leaned back in his chair. All his hard work was finally paying off. He had steady work and he could pick and chose the ones he wanted to work on and not just take anything. His business was great.

But his personal life? The smile slipped from his face. Without Rush, none of it would mean a damn thing, and right now, with Rush in Spring Lake and him in Houston, it looked as if he'd have to settle for weekends with a man who was deeply closeted.

Brian knew he could never be fully in Rush's life, not if Rush stayed at the ranch. He understood the small-town mentality and its irrational fear of gays, but he knew he could never go back into the closet, not even for Rush. Those days were over. The thought of hiding his love for Rush made his stomach clench, but the thought of not being at Rush's side every morning hurt worse.

Life would be easier for them in Houston. Here, in The Montrose, gay men lived openly. Brian still felt the prejudice of others, but it was a small part of his life, and he dealt with it by his actions. He refused to be a stereotype. He was merely a man who happened to find other men sexually attractive.

Spring Lake and the Double T were a hell of a long way from Montrose.

However, he'd never ask Rush to give up something he so clearly loved. That ranch was a part of Rush, of his heritage, of what made Rush, Rush. And it was part of what had made Brian fall in love with the big cowboy.

Going to the kitchen for a beer, he decided all he could do right now was to hope Rush could find the strength to come out.

Brian dropped a wedge of lime into his Corona and took a swallow.

How long could they keep their love alive across the distance that separated their worlds?

* * *

Rush sat on the porch, his feet on the railing, and sipped his beer. He hadn't stopped smiling for days. The memory of Brian, of what had happened between them in his backyard under the stars was too good to let go. He'd dwell in it every chance he'd get until they were together again.

Maybe this weekend, Brian could come to the ranch. He'd love to show him around. They could go riding down to the creek. Make love under the stars again. The thought of

Brian's naked body stretched out again in the moonlight got his dick stiff in record time. He smiled as he imagined what his father would have said if he'd known Rush was sitting in his chair with a hard-on for another man.

The screen door opened, and Manuel stepped out.

"Going to call it a day, Rush." The Double T's foreman wiped his lined face with a blue kerchief and tucked it back into the pocket of his jeans. "The men finished replacing the fence. I figured they could move onto that new corral behind the barn you'd been wanting. For the quarter horses."

"Sounds good. Tomorrow before you come out, order the supplies you'll need at Wilson's." Rush took another sip and rested the bottle on his hip to hide the bulge in his jeans.

The old stared at him and shook his head. "I don't know who she is, but some filly's got you grinning like a bearcat."

Rush shifted in his father's chair. His chair now. "There's no filly. I don't know what you're talking about."

"You sure? 'Cause you got that I-just-got-laid look all over your face."

"Shit, Manuel. Who'd want an old, beat-up cowboy like me?"

"Only half the married women in this town and all the unmarried ones," Manuel laughed.

"You're mistaken." His tone was sharper than it needed to be.

The older man snorted. "Fine. Keep it a secret. I'll find out soon enough. It'll be all over town by the end of the week, anyway."

Rush cleared his throat and crossed his legs at the ankles. Manuel's shot may have been close, but he hadn't scored a bull's eye.

"There's nothing to tell, nothing to find out, Manuel." He pulled his voice back to normal. "Same old, same old."

"Right." Manuel walked down the steps, then turned and looked at him. "Rush, whoever it is, I'm glad. In all the years I've known you, I don't think I've ever seen you so happy." Then he turned and headed to his old pickup truck, got in, and drove off.

Rush doubted Manuel would be happy for him if he knew the truth. The old cowboy had worked for Rush's father for years and was one of the few hands he'd kept on after his father's death. Rush was pretty sure his foreman had the same prejudices as his father. Telling him about his male lover was not an option.

Manuel had gotten one thing right. The whole fucking town would know he was gay once they saw him and Brian together.

There was no way in hell Brian could ever come to the ranch.

* * *

Wednesday night the phone rang at nine p.m. sharp. Rush snatched it off the bedside table and flipped it open. He'd been waiting for the call from Brian all week and thought it would never come. He was tired of jerking off without Brian's deep voice urging him on.

"Rush?" Brian's voice filled him up and settled him deeper into the bed as he stroked his hardened prick.

"Darlin'. Been waiting for your call."

"Have you? How have you been passing the time?"

"With my hand on my dick, thinking of you and me and those stars overhead as I fucked your ass last Friday. How about you?" Rush smeared the precum across the tip of his cock and shuddered.

"Damn, cowboy. I've been jerking off every morning in the shower, and every night in bed, calling out your name."

"I'm here now, darlin'. Talk to me. Tell me what you want me to do to you."

Brian sighed into the phone. "I want your dick so far up my ass you'll tickle my tonsils."

"Fuck, yeah." Rush pulled hard on his dick, his balls already burning in their need to unload.

"I want your big balls slapping my ass, your strong hands holding me down, making me take what you give me. I want you to do it hard and fast and angry."

"Angry, huh? Your ass needs some pounding?" Shit, he'd explode in a minute if Brian kept this up.

"Yeah, it does. Make me scream, lover."

"It'll be my pleasure. You like that I'm bigger than you, don't you? You want me to handle you, dominate you, huh?" That idea made Rush's dick throb even harder.

"Fuck, yeah. I'm yours, lover, and I want you to show me who's boss."

"I'm boss, darlin'. Say it, Brian. I'm the boss."

"You're the boss, Rush." Brian's words caused precum to dribble from the slit in Rush's prick, and he used the glistening droplets to glide his hand over his heated flesh. It was so delicious. He squeezed tighter, fucking his own hand. Not as good as fucking Brian, but it would do for now.

"I'll fuck you whenever I want, right?" he rasped.

"Whenever, lover."

"Are you close?"

"Fuck, yeah."

"Are you leaking?" He stroked faster as his balls pulled up to his body.

"Like a faucet, lover."

"Good. Is it all over your hands?"

"Coating them."

"Lick it off, darlin'. Taste yourself and tell me what it's like."

"You know how it tastes."

"I'm the boss. Do it."

Rush could hear Brian moaning as he licked his fingers. "Fuck, it's salty, a little bitter. Not as good as cum. I love the way your cum tastes when it's shooting down my throat."

Rush moaned and raised his hand to his lips. He flicked out his tongue and licked between his fingers. Salty, and thinner than real cum.

"You're doing it, too, aren't you? Bastard. The vision of you licking your cum from your fingers…you're going to make me come." Brian moaned.

"Me? If you don't stop that sweet little moan you do, I'm going to blow my load."

"Christ, lover. It's coming." Brian panted. "I can't stop it. Don't want to stop it."

"Don't, darlin'. Say my name."

"Rush, oh God, Rush, I love you." Brian's groan was joined by Rush's as he exploded. Hot, ropey cum splattered over Rush's belly as he shuddered.

Hearing Brian say he loved him had made him lose control.

Rush closed his eyes. "If you ever cheat on me, Brian, I don't know what I'd do."

"I'll never cheat. You've got my dick in the palm of your hand along with my heart."

"I don't know if I could take it, you know."

"I know. I feel the same. You're the only man for me, lover."

"I only want you." Rush still couldn't say it, couldn't manage to get those three little words out of his mouth and past his lips. They seemed to die somewhere between his heart and his tongue.

"I need you, lover. This weekend?"

Rush froze. "Your place?"

"I was hoping I could come out to the ranch some time."

"That's not going to happen, Brian. I'm not out here, and you know that." Rush ran his fingertip through the cooling cum on his belly, painting Brian's name on his skin.

"I know. I can't force you out, and I don't want to. When you're ready, you'll do it."

Rush fell silent. How the hell could he tell Brian there was a very good chance that would never happen? Instead, he waited for Brian to offer his place.

Brian cleared his throat. "Okay, come here. Can you at least stay the weekend?"

"No. I have to get back on Saturday."

"Get one of the hands to do the chores." Rush could hear the disbelief in Brian's tone.

Rush sighed. He could get Manuel to do it, but he was already suspicious and he'd just ask too many questions. Who else did he trust? Ricky, maybe. "Okay, I'll see what I can do, but no promises."

"Okay. If it happens, it happens. But we have a date on Friday night, right?"

"Right."

"You're staying all night, right?" Brian sounded pissed off.

"Right. Those are your rules," Rush bit out.

"If you want my ass, those are the rules. Just say the word, cowboy, and we don't have to do this at all." Now, Rush could hear the anger in Brian's voice, and his own temper flared.

He almost said fuck it, but his need and desire for Brian zipped his lips shut, preventing the smart-ass remark from slipping out. For once, he wouldn't ruin things.

Brian sighed. "I don't want to fight, Rush. I want to make love to you, make you moan, make you cry out my name. I don't want to cause you pain." His voice was like gravel as his emotions came through the phone loud and clear.

"I don't want to fight, either." Rush relented. "Want to make you scream, darlin'."

"You will. You always do."

"Night, Brian. See you on Friday."

"Night, Rush. Can't wait." Brian hung up.

Rush closed the phone, put it on the nightstand, then got up to take a shower. He knew he'd have to take another one in the morning, after he whacked off.

Tomorrow, he'd do it in the shower and kill two birds with his right hand.

Rush turned the knobs and needling hot water burst out. He stepped under it and rinsed the dried cum off his stomach, then from his cock and balls.

Turning around, he leaned over, propped against the tile wall with his hand, and let the water beat on his shoulders and back.

Brian's face appeared behind Rush's closed eyes, and his hand went straight to his dick like a fucking homing pigeon.

It sprang to life much too quickly. Rush spilled against the glass wall of the shower, painting it with his cream and crying out for Brian.

Chapter Fifteen

"Is this Rose Mae Waters?" Brian swiveled side to side in his chair, tapping his fingers on the desk pad.

"Why, yes it is. Who's speaking?" a firm but aged voice answered.

"I'm calling about Lydia Mae Waters."

The silence on the other end of the line was thick enough to cut.

Brian cleared his throat. "Are you her mother?"

"Who is this?"

"My name is Brian Russell, ma'am. I'm a private investigator. Lydia's name has come up in a search I'm doing for a client."

"Lydia's dead."

"When did she die?" Brian moved quickly, snatching up a pen to take down the info. No surprise, he'd expected she was dead.

"Years ago," she sighed, sounding incredibly tired.

"Do you remember when?" Could a mother ever forget the date her child died? Brian didn't think so.

"Back in eighty-six. She was only nineteen." Now a palatable sadness overcame the woman's weariness.

"I'd like to meet with you. I have something to discuss with you, and I'd prefer not to do it over the phone."

More silence. A sigh. "All right." There was no mistaking her reluctance, but she'd still agreed.

"Is tomorrow fine with you, Mrs. Waters? Around ten a.m.?"

"That's fine. You've got my phone number, do you have my address?" The lady was sharp enough, it seemed.

"Yes. You're inside the 610 Loop, near Ella Boulevard, right?"

"That's right. See you at ten." She hung up.

Brian sat back. He'd wait until after his visit to inform Sammi of his progress.

* * *

He located the small Craftsman cottage with little difficulty. It was tidy, with a well-kept front garden. Behind the house, large oaks and a magnolia towered.

Brian opened the cast iron gate, walked up the sideway, and climbed the front steps. On the small porch, several cats, their bellies up, backs twisted, eyes closed, lounged in the late morning sun. Well, she was a cat person. Weren't most old women?

The lace curtains at the windows confirmed that this was an old lady's house. He wondered if the furniture would have those lace antimacassars draped over their backs and arms or if everything would smell like mothballs.

He rang the doorbell and waited.

The door opened, and a small woman with Sammi's deep brown eyes stared up at him.

"You must be Mr. Russell."

Brian held out his opened PI license case to her. "Yes, ma'am. May I come in?"

She glanced at it, sighed, and stepped back. "Might as well."

He entered the cozy room. No doilies on the overstuffed furniture, but they were covered in a quiet, flowered chintz, and the air was sweet with the smell of gingerbread.

She motioned to the couch and sat in a chair. On the low coffee table, a plate of cookies waited. "Can I offer you some iced tea?"

"That would be very nice, yes." Brian sat on the end of the couch, sinking into the cushions. His knees bumped the coffee table. Seemed she didn't have too many tall visitors.

The room was clean and neat. On the walls were a few scattered pictures. None of people, they were all generic landscapes and still lifes. He glanced around the room for family photos but didn't find any.

"So, what do you want to know about Lydia?" She carried a tray with two glasses of iced tea, a bowl of sugar, and two spoons and placed it on the small table between them.

"Mrs. Waters, did you know Lydia had a child before she died?" He watched her face for her reaction.

As she lifted a glass to him, she froze. Her eyes widened in surprise. "Lydia had a child?" He took the glass from her before she dropped it.

"Yes ma'am. A son. His name is…"

"I don't want to know his name." She cut him off, shaking her head.

Brian sat back and watched her. He'd have to go carefully. He'd given her an obvious shock, and from his experience, there was no telling what some people would do or say when that happened.

"All right. Can you give me some information about Lydia?"

"Why? This kid hire you to find me?" Her eyes narrowed.

"He hired me to find his family, yes."

"What's he want? Money?" She looked around the modest home. "I don't have any."

"No, ma'am. He just wants to learn about his family. Lydia gave him up with he was two years old."

Her head jerked up, but she remained quiet as she added a spoon of sugar to her tea and stirred it slowly.

"Mrs. Waters. Sammi was given up for adoption. That never happened, and he spent most of his life moving from one foster home to another."

Without looking up, she said, "What's wrong with him?"

Brian blinked. "Probably the same thing that was wrong with your daughter, Mrs. Waters." It was a chance, but he took it.

Mrs. Waters slumped back in her chair and ran her hand over her face. When she looked up, she looked much older than the mid-sixties he'd placed her. He waited for her to speak.

"Lydia was a difficult child. She tested us, me and Walter, my husband."

Brian nodded, encouraging her to continue. He decided not to pull out his BlackBerry to take notes, thinking it would hamper her in getting the story out.

"She was a lovely child, really. Small, petite like me, but with Walter's blue eyes. A real beauty. But troubled." She glanced at Brian and gave a quick smile.

"She heard voices?"

Her eyebrows rose, and then she nodded. "Yes. From the time she could first talk, she told me about the voices. Imaginary friends, I thought at first. But it was more." She bit her lip and halted.

"She could hear your thoughts."

She gasped and her hand clutched at her throat. "How did you know?"

"Like mother, like son." He shrugged.

"She ran away from home when she was fifteen." Her face crumpled, and her eyes welled with tears. "And we let her go. Never reported it. Walter didn't want her back."

"She scared him," Brian added.

"Yes." Tears spilled. "Imagine being afraid of your own child. He thought she was evil, as if the devil himself had taken our beautiful little girl and made a monster of her."

"How did you know about her death?"

"The police. They found her body. She had her driver's license in her purse."

"Can you tell me what happened?"

She took a long sip of her tea and then wiped her thin lips on a paper napkin.

"Suicide. She drove her car onto the 610 Loop, parked, got out, and jumped over the side. Hit the concrete road below." She'd repeated it as if reading from a newspaper, or the police report. "We had her buried in a cemetery on I-45, far from us. I had to fight Walter for that."

"He didn't want to claim her even after she'd died?"

She looked out the window. "He was a hard man," was all she said.

Sammi's life had been part of a larger tragedy going back in time to his mother. Even she had been a stranger, unwelcome in her own home.

"This young man. Sammi?"

"Yes. Samuel James Waters," he repeated the name on the birth certificate.

"Samuel. He hears voices, too?"

"Yes, but he's handled it well. Realized that he has a gift, not a curse. He's not a monster. He's…" Brian searched for a way to describe his best friend's lover. "He's decent, hard working, caring, and sensitive and determined."

She shook her head. "He wants to meet me?"

"He wanted only to know about his family. I told him that it was up to you whether or not he could contact you."

She grimaced as if she didn't believe him.

Brian leaned forward, hands grasped together. "It's the truth. I won't force you into it, and I won't give him any information about you, if you don't want me to."

She stood, signaling their meeting was over.

"I'll call you with my decision, Mr. Russell. In the meantime, please don't tell him any information about me until then."

Brian stood, and placed his tea on the tray. "I'm going to give him the info about his mother. He has a right to that."

She gave him a small nod, then walked him to the door.

Brian turned and extended his hand. "Thank you for seeing me, Mrs. Waters."

"Of course." She took his hand, clasped it briefly.

"And I'm sorry for your loss," he added.

She gave him a curt nod and shut the door.

He'd just have to wait for her call. In the meantime, he was going to look up Lydia Mae's death certificate.

He sat in his SUV outside Sammi's grandmother's house and considered his choices. He could search the newspapers for a report of Lydia's death, could go down to City Hall and repeat his earlier search, or he could go to the cemetery and look through their records.

He pulled out his BlackBerry and did a search on cemeteries on I-45. Lucky for him, there was only one. A day in a graveyard beat the hell out of an hour in City Hall. He started the engine and pulled away.

Forty minutes later, he pulled into the cemetery and drove down the black asphalt road to the large funeral home that held center stage. The grounds were well kept, with low rolling hillocks dotted with stone markers in neat rows. In the near distance, an open grave waited, a large green canopy beside it, and chairs set up in rows underneath.

There were quite a few cars in the parking lot. He found a space in the rear, parked and made his way to the front of the building. Brian opened the door and stepped into quiet darkness, his feet sinking into thick carpet. Somewhere, muffled organ music played. His eyes adjusted to the dim lighting. The place was as cold as a meat locker.

At the office, he spoke in quiet tones to a young woman in a two-piece suit, her blonde hair pulled back into a tight bun.

"I want to locate someone buried here in the eighties."

She motioned him to take the chair in front of her desk. "If you tell me the name of the deceased, I'll try to locate it for you." She spoke slowly and sympathetically, the way one does to people who are bereaved over the loss of a loved one.

"Lydia Mae Waters. Died, 1986."

"Let me see what I can find." She swung over to her computer and typed. Her nails were short, unpolished, and neat. No overworked sigh, no rapid typing. Her movements were slower, as if her typing showed the same respect for the dead as her lowered voice.

It must be hell to spend your whole day whispering. At the end of her day, did she get in her car, crank up the stereo and sing to it at the top of her lungs?

"Here we go. Lydia Mae Waters. Section thirty-four, row fifteen, marker three." She handed him a map of the cemetery. "If you follow the main road to the back, turn at the first left and go straight. You'll see the section markers."

He stood, brochure in hand. "Thank you."

"My pleasure. And my condolences." She gave him a sad smile, probably the same one she gave everyone who came in here.

He imagined her going home, changing into something other than the plain black suit she wore, and going out to a bar, where she could dance and laugh the night away. He hoped her life was more exciting than this.

He got back in the SUV, and followed her instructions. Minutes later, he parked, got out and counted off the rows, then counted the markers.

Lydia Mae Waters

Born August 23, 1969

Died November 2, 1986

That was all. No "Beloved Child of…" No "Rest in Everlasting Peace."

Brian's eyes teared and his throat constricted. He hoped that when his time came, there would be more on his marker than his birth and death dates. That someone would care enough about him to remark on his passing that he would be missed and was once loved.

He lowered his head, said a brief prayer for Lydia, and left.

Chapter Sixteen

"I'm sorry Sammi. The most I can tell you is what I've already told you about your mother." Brian tapped his pencil against the keyboard of his computer.

"But this woman. My grandmother..." Sammi's voice faded. "She doesn't want to see me? Ever?"

Brian's heat broke for the kid. "That's not what she said, Sammi. She needs time to think about this. It's a lot to take in all at once."

"I understand. I would probably remind her of my mother. It would probably dredge up a lot of bad memories." Damn, Sammi, but he was always so sensitive about other people's feelings. Must be due to hearing so many thoughts, and feeling all those emotions.

If it had been him, Brian would have railed about the old woman's selfishness.

But Sammi had been abandoned by the ones who were supposed to love and care for him his entire life, so he was probably used to it. Then he'd met and fallen in love with Mitchell, the only person ever to go back for Sammi, the only one who believed that Sammi was worth fighting for.

"That may be part of it, but give her time, Sammi. She might surprise you and come around."

"I have so many questions I want to ask her about my mother. Do you think she knew who my father was?"

"I don't know. And Sammi?" Brian couldn't let any false hopes build inside Sammi; it would be too cruel. "You may never get that sort of information."

"I know. Thanks for everything, Brian. You did a great job. Drop by and give me the bill for all the work you've done, okay?"

"Sure. Tell Mitchell hi for me."

"Will do. Bye." Sammi hung up.

Brian swore, closed his phone, and tossed it on the desk. Damn, he'd wanted this to turn out good for Sammi, he really did, but it seemed as if the cards had been stacked against the young man from the beginning.

The alarm chirped on his desktop, and an alert popped up.

Dinner with Rush in two hours.

Time to get ready for his date. Brian pushed out of his chair and headed for his bedroom, whistling as he walked down the hall. He reached his room and undressed.

He stepped under the hot shower, stopped whistling, and started scrubbing. After getting clean and a fresh shave, he changed the sheets on the bed and put the bottle of Spanish sparkling wine he'd bought in the wine cooler to chill.

Soon, Rush would be in his arms and in his bed. Nothing was going to ruin his plans for tonight.

* * *

Rush checked himself in the mirror. His second "date" with Brian was only two hours away, but this night had taken what seemed like ages to get here. His clothes were fine, and this time, he'd wear his hat. The truck was spotless, inside and out.

Everything was perfect.

Almost everything. This was only their second meeting, and already he knew he couldn't stand being away from Brian. How could this continue, with him at the ranch and the man he loved in Houston?

His mind circled its wagons around their problem of distance.

Liar. It's your problem, not Brian's.

Brian was out, openly gay. It was Rush's fear of discovery that kept them apart, that ruined all of it, that would leave him heartbroken and ultimately alone.

Manuel came up to the truck and leaned against the side. "Off to Houston again?"

"Yep." Rush tried not to blush as he got in.

"Didn't you go last week?" Manuel lit a cigarette and blew smoke from between smiling lips.

"Yep."

"Truck all shiny and damned if you don't look good enough to go to church."

"So?" Rush barked as he tossed his hat on the seat next to him.

"So. Must be one hell of a woman." He shook his gray head.

"I told you, there's no woman," Rush growled. "And besides, it's none of your damned business what I'm doing."

Manuel's eyebrows shot up and he held his hands up in placation. "Okay, boss, okay." He stepped away from the truck.

Rush slammed the truck into reverse and shot backward, spun the wheel, and tore down the road in a haze of dust, leaving Manuel scratching and shaking his head.

"Shit!" That had been close. He'd really lost it back there, yelling at his foreman. Manuel didn't deserve that treatment. Feeling guilty and hating it, he vowed to apologize to the old man on Monday. He hated feeling guilty about seeing Brian and it shouldn't ever feel bad, but lying about it sucked.

Even when he'd gone to Houston all those times before, he'd never lied about it. Just told Manuel he'd be gone Friday evening and that was that. It hadn't mattered because he hadn't cared about those other men.

Now, he cared. He cared a whole lot and it was scary as shit.

Rush settled back in the seat, punched up some music, and tried to forget about the ranch and the narrow minds of Spring Lake. He was heading to Houston to have dinner with the man of his dreams and damn it, he was going to enjoy every moment he and Brian had together.

Before they were just a memory.

* * *

Hoping it was Rush, Brian opened the door. It was early, but he didn't care.

"Mitchell? What brings you here?" he greeted his best friend.

Mitchell barged past him.

"Why don't you come in?" Brian said to the air. Then he shut the door and followed Mitchell into the living room. Mitchell paced the length of the room and then threw himself into a chair.

"How could you do that to Sammi?" The look on Mitchell's face was etched agony.

"Do what?" Brian blinked.

"Tell him that he had a family and then not tell him who or where they were?" Mitchell glared at him, anger burning in his eyes.

Brian sighed. "Mitchell, you know how it goes. I can find them, but if they don't want to be contacted, I have to respect that."

"But it's Sammi, damn it." Mitchell hit his fist on his thigh.

"I know who hired me." Brian's voice lowered as he struggled to keep it under control. No sense in both of them going off. "And by the way, that's confidential information." He sat on the end of the couch near Mitchell.

"Sammi told me." Mitchell looked up, defensiveness in his eyes.

"I'm sure he did. Is he really upset?" Brian reached out a hand and touched Mitchell's knee. Mitchell's hand reached out and closed over his.

"He's devastated. He won't talk about it, but I can tell." He swiped his hand through his thick brown hair.

"I'll bet. That kind of emotion must be very strong."

Mitchell shook his head. "No, that's not it. It's worse. He's cut me off."

"What?" Brian sat up. "Cut you off, how?"

"It's like that time with Donovan. He's cut his emotions off. I can't feel him anymore. I can't hear his thoughts, his desires." Mitchell looked bleak, and it tore Brian's heart to think of the pain his best friend was going through.

"He's only trying to protect you."

"I know. He's so… so…" Mitchell's words failed.

"Yeah. He loves you so much, Mitchell."

Mitchell slumped. "He doesn't understand how his trying to protect me hurts me." He rubbed his chest over his heart as if there were an actual pain centered there and Brian wondered if Mitchell really did feel a physical pain.

"Then tell him," Brian urged softly.

"I tried to. He just said he had to go to work and left. Damn it, Brian, just tell me the woman's name. Maybe I can go talk to her, make her see. Make her understand how much Sammi needs her," Mitchell begged, his hand tightening on Brian's hand.

"I can't do that and you know it."

"You're my best friend. Help me. Just this time."

It was a hard decision and a bad place to be, caught between his best friend and his personal code of ethics.

“Please don’t put me in this spot.” He hated being forced into a corner.

“Not even for me?” Mitchell stood, his hands in fists, and for a moment, Brian wondered if they would come to blows over this.

Fuck, this sucked, but there was no way he could give Mitchell what he wanted and not lose a piece of his own self-respect.

“No.” Brian shook his head.

Every muscle in Mitchell’s body tensed, and he shook with the strain of either fury or control, Brian didn’t know which. Then Mitchell collapsed back into the chair, his head in his hands.

“Goddamn, shit, crap, fuck!”

Brian knelt beside him and wrapped an arm around his shoulders. “It sucks. But I know you understand, baby.” His words were soft and soothing, trying to comfort.

Mitchell lifted his sweat dampened face, and wiped it with the sleeve of his shirt. “You don’t know how much it hurts. It’s like part of me has been torn off. He’s so far away from me, so unreachable.”

“He’ll be back.” There was nothing else Brian could say without sounding patronizing. “He loves you. Adores you, actually.” He chuckled.

Mitchell smiled. “Yeah, I know he does. That’s why he’s doing it, to protect me.”

Brian stood. “Come on. Go home to your man. Even if he won’t let you feel him, he still needs you there.”

Mitchell stood. "You're right. Damn, I should have married you ages ago. How did I let you get away?" He laughed and punched Brian playfully in the arm.

Rush turned the corner onto Brian's street and it felt like coming home. All he'd thought about for the last hour had been slipping into Brian's arms. Then slipping into his body. He shuddered at the thought, and his cock stiffened in already too-tight blue jeans.

He pulled up and parked the truck on the street. A black Jetta was parked in the driveway behind Brian's Tahoe. He got out, gave it a quick once-over, and walked up the sidewalk to the porch.

The door opened and a man stepped out, with Brian right behind him.

"Thanks, Brian. I'll see you later." The man slipped into Brian's arms, and they hugged.

Rush's foot froze on the bottom step and his stomach dropped out from under him as his world was ripped away. He wanted to shout, "Get your fucking hands of my man" but instead he barked, "What the hell?"

The men jumped apart.

Rush took another step up the stairs, fists clenched, white-hot anger boiling through his veins. What a fool he'd been. What a fucking asshole. Brian was two-timing him with this guy after he'd sworn he'd never cheat.

"Rush!" Brian grinned at him.

Did Brian think he was an idiot? Rush caught him red-handed, and he was laughing? How dare he laugh? The urge to punch Brian's lights out surged through him. He'd beat the crap out of that smug, good-looking bastard with his hands on Brian while he was at it.

The man stepped back and looked him up and down, assessing him. The guy was big, but not as big as he was. Rush advanced on the men as fury poured through his body, and his heart galloped like a team of runaway horses.

Brian stepped between the men. "Rush. Stop! This is Mitchell. My best friend."

Rush froze. Shit. It was his worst nightmare. The guy from Brian's fantasies. The man he wanted but wouldn't touch for fear of losing his friendship. Well, they were sure as hell touching just then. Lies. It had all been lies.

Mitchell held out his hand for Rush to shake. Was he fucking for real?

"Brian's told me so much about you. Glad to finally meet you?"

"Yeah? What did he say? What a fool I am? How easy it was to play me? You two have a good laugh about it?" Rush growled, letting Mitchell's hand hang in the air.

"What?" Mitchell looked at Brian.

"It's not like that, Rush. I told you, we're not together, never have been." Brian tried to reassure him, but Rush wasn't falling for that load of bullshit.

"You looked pretty damned together just now."

"I know it sounds clichéd, but it's not what you think," Mitchell said.

Rush glared at him. "You, shut up. This is between me and Brian."

"Hey, don't tell him to shut up. He's right. Nothing is going on between us. I had no idea you were so jealous, Rush." Brian shouldn't sound so shocked. Hell, what did the man expect him to feel?

"Kind of flattering, if it wasn't so wrong." Mitchell chuckled.

"Yeah. Guess he hasn't told you about the fantasies?" Rush shot back.

"Fantasies?" Mitchell's eyebrows rose. "What fantasies, Brian?"

Brian gasped and looked as if he wanted to disappear into a hole in the ground.

"The ones about you and him and his backyard," Rush blurted.

"Rush! I told you that in confidence." Brian grimaced as the red in his cheeks deepened.

"A fantasy about me? Did you jerk off to it?" Mitchell asked. "Brian, I feel so cheap, so dirty. I like it." His wicked grin and sparkling eyes just added fuel to the fray.

"Fuck, I'm so sorry." Brian didn't seem to know who to reach out to, Mitchell or Rush, and Rush didn't know who he was apologizing to either.

"That's okay. If we're being honest, I've had a few about you myself." Mitchell waggled his eyebrows at Brian.

"What?" Brian yelped and blushed even redder. "Mitchell, now is not the time for smart-ass remarks," he pleaded.

"Look, if you two have something going on that needs to be explored, say it now, and don't waste any more of my time." Rush was so pissed he could spit, but he'd be damned if he'd continue to be the butt of their jokes.

Brian ignored Rush's ire, stepped up to him, and cupped his chin. "Cowboy, look at me. Look in my eyes and read my lips. I love you, Rush. You. Not Mitchell. There's a big difference between what I feel for him and what I feel for you. And what I want to do with you. For a long, long time to come."

God, Rush wanted to believe that more than anything in the world.

"But those fantasies?"

"Hey, can he help it? I'm a great guy," Mitchell interjected. "So is he. We may think about it, but we've never done anything about it. Besides, I'm already soul bonded to another man. If I cheated, Sammi would know, and then he'd have to kill me."

"Soul bonded?" Rush frowned. What the hell was he talking about?

Mitchell grinned. "We can hear each other's thoughts, feel each other's emotions."

Rush stared at him, then shot his eyes over to Brian, who seemed to be taking this just fine. "Right."

"It's true," Brian said. "I might as well tell you. I'd have to get around to it eventually. Mitchell and Sammi have hyperdeveloped… I don't know. Empathic abilities. They can and do share their thoughts and feelings. I've seen it. I believe it."

Rush looked at Mitchell. He looked like a regular guy. An incredibly handsome guy. His jealousy flared, then died down. Hell, he could see in the dark, didn't that make them sort of the same? The idea that there were other people with some sort of super powers had never occurred to him. He'd always thought he was the only one who was weird. A freak of nature.

Mitchell elbowed Brian. "Tell him about your powers, Brian."

Rush held his breath as his eyes darted back to his lover. "Powers?"

"I have hunches, premonitions, I suppose. I know when something is going to happen, whether people are telling the truth, stuff like that. Not always, but when it counts, it comes to me." Brian looked into Rush's eyes. "I know it sounds weird, but I've had this ability since I was a kid."

"You know when things are going to happen." He turned and pointed to Mitchell. "And you and your partner can hear and feel each other." Rush shook his head. And he thought he was odd. He opened his mouth to say, "You ain't seen nothing yet," and tell of his own odd ability, but something made him snap it shut and keep the secret locked inside.

"Whether you believe it or not, I hope this won't affect how you feel about me," Brian asked. He touched Rush's face again. "I'm not crazy."

"I can deal with it." Rush nodded and Brian exhaled.

"Well, now that that's settled, I'm off." Mitchell headed down the steps. "Look. Don't tell Sammi about the fantasy thing. Please." He gave Rush a look that said, "I trust you, trust me."

Rush gave him a nod.

Brian grinned. "Don't tell me you're scared of Sammi?"

"Of hurting him, yes. Of him leaving me?" Mitchell shrugged. "We're bonded, Brian. If either of us leaves, the other dies." Then he went to his car, got in, and started it. With a final wave, he backed out of the drive and left.

"Shit. Is he for real?" Rush ran his hand through his hair and stared after the Jetta.

"Yeah, he is." Brian frowned. "I never knew you were so jealous, cowboy."

"Neither did I, but when I saw you with your arms around another man, I went berserk. I'm sorry." Rush looked deep into Brian's brown eyes and the fire between them ignited.

They came together on the porch, arms wrapped around firm bodies, and hungry mouths met and fought for dominance of the kiss.

When they broke apart, both of them were panting.

"Fuck, darlin', don't ever do that again. My heart can't stand it." Rush leaned his head against Brian's forehead. The depth of his anger, his boiling jealousy, his absolute terror that he'd lost Brian had rocked him to his very core.

"Never." Brian kissed him again. "Now, what do you want for dinner?"

"Do you have to ask?" Rush pulled him through the open door of the house and threw Brian against the wall, pinning him with his hands around Brian's wrists.

"Dessert first?" Brian whispered as Rush's stiff cock rubbed against his.

"Oh, yeah, darlin'. I want to eat my dessert first."

Then he let Brian's hands go and fell to his knees.

Chapter Seventeen

Before Brian could get the first word out of his mouth, Rush had flipped open the button of Brian's jeans, drawn down the zipper, and pulled his cock out of his pants. It ached, and where Rush touched it, the ache was soothed, first by his hands and then, to Brian's mind-blowing pleasure, by Rush's mouth.

Using the flat of his tongue, Rush laved the underside of Brian's prick, taking long, loving strokes up and down the length of it. Brian watched as Rush's head dipped, and the scrape of Rush's glorious tongue on Brian's balls made him shudder.

"Fuck, cowboy, do that again," he whimpered. Locking his knees, he pressed farther back into the wall to keep himself upright.

Rush captured one choice nut in his mouth, swirled his tongue around it, and then sucked it completely inside. Brian groaned in the sheer ecstasy of it. Nothing had ever felt so good to Brian than having Rush touch him, suck him, and love him.

Moving to the other side, Rush repeated the sweet torture and Brian wrapped his fingers in that tawny mane, and pulled him closer.

"Suck me, lover."

Rush complied, taking him deep into his mouth. Brian's balls tightened, and the urge to unload climbed from the pit of his groin and built like water rising behind a dam. He'd burst any minute. Not knowing how much more he could stand, he was more than willing to test his control.

"That's it. Use that incredible tongue of yours." He glanced down.

Somewhere in all of this, Rush had freed himself and was using his other hand to jerk himself off while sucking off Brian.

Fuck, that just turned Brian on even more, and the dam cracked.

"Shit, I'm going to come. Watching you do yourself, fuck, it's so sexy, so hot."

Rush pulled away, his lips still resting on the tip of Brian's dick. "Want you now. Turn around."

Brian obeyed. Rush's hand parted the globes of his ass as he spit, moistened his cock and then pushed it into Brian's tight hole.

"Gonna fuck you against this wall, darlin'," the cowboy growled.

Brian spread his legs and pressed his hands against the wall to better angle his ass upward, to give Rush's dick access to what it sought. There was a buildup of pressure, a sharp sting, and then Rush was inside him.

"Oh, goddamn, it's so hot inside you. So fucking tight. God, I love fucking you."

Brian's ass was full of Rush, and the first withdrawal left him gasping. Then the pounding started. Rush was like an animal in rut, uncontrollable, passionate. His hands covered Brian's as he held him.

This is what Brian had longed for. Being taken, being forced to take what Rush gave him. He'd always wanted a mindless, ass-banging, angry caveman fuck. Tonight, against this wall, he was getting exactly what he'd dreamed of.

And it was better than he'd ever imagined.

His cock, still erect, battered against the slightly rough wall, and sent waves of pleasure through his loins. His balls slapped the wall, rubbing and pressing, bringing him off. The harsh scrape and rasp of Rush plundering his ass drove him to the brink.

When Rush took his shoulder in his mouth and bit down, Brian lost it.

"Oh God," he cried out, shooting his load upward, smearing it on the wall and his belly, as his ass clenched with each eruption.

Taking Rush with him.

"Sweet Jesus. Sweet Jesus." Rush sobbed against his back.

Their hands wove together, bloodless knuckles showing the force of their grips, the nameless need each of them felt marking the wall beneath them.

Panting, they rested against each other, holding themselves upright until Rush's cock slipped from its home and he broke their contact.

Brian shuddered at the sudden coldness, then peeled himself off the wall.

Rush returned with a towel and helped clean Brian and the wall. Neither of them could speak just yet. Brian didn't have any idea of what to say after that amazing merging. Mere words would be inadequate. Maybe, if he were a poet...

Rush looked into his eyes, cupped his chin and leaned in for a kiss. Tender, soft, gentle, it was everything their coupling hadn't been, and it was perfect.

Brian rested his chin in that calloused hand and closed his eyes. Moments later, Rush's lips found his and lingered, just pressing, nothing more.

After rearranging clothes, they made it to the kitchen, and Brian pulled two beers from the fridge. The good wine would wait. They twisted off the caps and downed the beer in long, thirst-driven gulps.

"How about that dinner?" Brian asked.

"Starving. Lead the way." Rush grinned at him.

"Steaks?"

"I'm always ready for some good beef." Rush nodded and tossed his bottle into the trash.

Brian took the last swallow and threw his in, the glass clinking in the wastebasket.

"Let's take the Tahoe."

They left the house, got in the SUV and backed out of the drive. On Montrose, Brian turned toward Westhiemer.

"Where to?" Rush had rolled the window down, and the fresh air tossed his blond hair around. Brian glanced over at him and felt a swell of pride in his lover. Rush was one hell of a sexy man, and he was all his.

"The Cattleman's Club. Best aged prime beef in town."

They drove to the restaurant, holding hands, heads bobbing to the country music on the radio. They discovered they both loved George Strait, Toby Keith, and Keith Urban.

"Guess I'm a cowboy at heart," Brian said.

Rush had reached over and tousled his hair. "A wannabe cowboy, city boy."

"Maybe. But I lassoed the real thing." Brian grinned at him.

Rush sat back, a smile on his face that Brian was more than happy to think of as satisfied.

At the restaurant, they sat in a red leather-upholstered booth across from each other. The place had dark gleaming woodwork, white linen tablecloths, and antique cowboy paraphernalia on the walls. They ordered T-bones, baked potatoes all the way, fried okra, and topped it all off with a basket of corn bread and rolls. The conversation was easy going and relaxed as they kidded with each other and told stories.

When the bill came, Brian reached for it. "You got the last one, cowboy. This one's mine." Rush nodded.

Then they were out in the night air, back in Brian's car and heading down Westheimer. "Ever been to the Water Wall?"

Rush shook his head. "I haven't really seen much of the sights in Houston, to tell the truth."

"It's very romantic. Everyone in Houston goes there on dates."

"Can't be as romantic as your backyard."

"Well, maybe not. Let me know what you think."

In a few minutes, he'd parked the car and they walked over to the huge fountain. Between the lights that illuminated it and the roar of the water as it fell from over two stories high, it was a truly magical place.

They stood together, holding hands. Around them, couples, both straight and gay, moved in and out of the light as they admired the fountain. In one corner, a man in a tuxedo got down on his knee in front of a beautifully gowned young woman and presented her with a ring. Everyone clapped when she'd nodded yes, her words lost in the sounds of the falls.

Brian squeezed Rush's hand and got a responding pressure.

Rush leaned down and kissed him. It was brief, but it was the first kiss they'd shared in public that Rush had instigated. Brian's heart leaped at the thought that Rush had become so relaxed and open in showing his feelings. Maybe, just maybe, he'd want more. And he'd want it bad enough to muster the courage Brian knew it would take for Rush to come out.

But he didn't spoil the moment with words. The gleam in Rush's eyes was enough for him. They strolled side by side back to the Tahoe, climbed in, and headed home.

When they got back to Brian's, there was no rush, no heated hurry to get to naked. They both knew it would happen and they both seemed to want to take their time.

Brian slipped under the covers and pressed his naked body against Rush's naked body, the soft pull of hair against hair on muscled, firm arms and legs was delicious. They warmed each other, heated flesh pressed together, hands slowly caressed and teased, and lips worshiped foreheads, throats, shoulders, fingertips.

That night they made love, slow and easy, Rush beneath Brian, Brian rocking lazy and steady into Rush as if he had all the time in the world to give his man. As if morning would never get there. As if Rush would never have to get out of Brian's bed and leave.

At last, when they'd both found sweet shuddering release in each other's arms, Brian lay with his head on Rush's shoulder, as one of the cowboy's hands stroked his arm, and he smoked a cigarette with the other.

"Tell me about your family." Brian broke the silence.

Rush shrugged beneath him. "Not much to tell. Everyone's dead." A stream of gray smoke rose in a column above the bed.

Brian raised his head and looked into Rush's eyes. "I'm sorry, love. Were you an only child?"

"My father wished so." He gave an angry grunt and took a deep drag. "I had a brother, Robert. We called him Robbie. He was the apple of my father's eye." The tone was bitter, and Brian didn't have to be a detective to know there was a story in there somewhere. He'd have to be careful and tease it out of the big man. Big he may be, but he was skittish, new to all this sharing of feelings.

"Younger?"

"Yeah. By four years."

"How'd he die?"

"Like a true Weston." Rush blew smoke rings, each one a perfect O.

Brian waited for the rest of it. It would come when Rush was ready. He'd been so talkative the entire evening that Brian had hoped it would continue.

"Robbie was a bronc rider. He was nineteen. He died doing what he loved."

"Jesus. Were you there?"

Rush flicked his ashes into the small bowl Brian had provided, and then took another drag. "Yep. We all were. He was going for the championship buckle."

"Can you tell me what happened, or is it too hard?"

Rush bit his lip, then blew out the smoke from the corner of his mouth.

"The horse he'd drawn was really rank. That means badass. A real kicker who'd stomp your guts out if it could. Robbie made the eight seconds but couldn't get free of the rope. He hung on, his feet dragging in the dirt, until the horse took a huge leap, twisted, and came down on its side. It crushed Robbie. He was dead before we could get to him." He crushed his cigarette out with an angry twist and a hard-blown plume of smoke.

"Christ, Rush, that's awful." Brian felt sick to his stomach. To have watched his brother be killed must have been horrific.

Rush's eyes closed and Brian could see traces of tears trapped in his long blond lashes. He wanted to kiss them away, but kept still, waiting for Rush to get it all out.

"When my dad realized Robbie was dead and he'd been left with me"— he shook his head— "I could see it in his eyes," he whispered.

"See what," Brian whispered back.

"He wished it had been me." Rush's jaw worked as he struggled with those words and God only knew what other demons that plagued him.

"Son of a bitch, baby." Brian snuggled deeper into Rush and squeezed him tighter, trying to give him comfort and not knowing what to do or say.

"It's okay."

"Okay? Fuck, Rush. You're telling me your father wished you'd been killed and you say it's okay?"

"It's 'cause I'm gay. He knew. I told him when I was seventeen."

"He didn't approve I take it." Brian tried to keep the bitterness out of his voice, but it wasn't easy. How could someone hate their own child for something so stupid as who they found attractive or who they fell in love with?

"He beat the crap out of me and told me if I ever gave him reason to think about what I'd told him again, he'd either kill me or kick me off the ranch." Rush's grip on Brian tightened. His naked need for love and acceptance clawed at Brian's heart.

"Shit." Brian held Rush, and neither of them spoke again.

Rush's breathing steadied, slowed and in a while, he snored softly. Brian turned out the light and pulled the covers over Rush's shoulders.

Brian understood now.

Rush had been in the closet his whole life, and the one time he'd tried to come out, he'd been slapped back inside so hard and so fast that he'd given up any hope of ever seeing the light on the other side of that closed door. Add to that, the guilt he must feel over Robbie's death and his father's disappointment.

Rush's father was dead. There was no need to for him to hide anymore.

But how in the world would Brian be able to convince Rush?

Chapter Eighteen

Rush's phone rang. He groaned, rolled over, and reached for it, slapping his hand on the bedside table. He found it, flipped it open, and held it to his ear.

"Weston," he muttered.

"Boss, it's Ricky. That mare's going to foal today, you better get back." At first, Rush didn't recognize the young man's slight accent, then his eyes snapped open.

"What's wrong with her?"

"She's down. I called the vet. He's coming out as soon as he can, but he's on another call."

"Call Manuel, get him there."

"Already did. He's on his way."

"Good. I'll be there as soon as I can, but it won't be for at least two hours." In the time it would take him to drive back to the ranch from Houston, she could have the foal or die during a difficult birth. He had a lot of time and money wrapped up in this foal, and he didn't want to lose either the mother or the baby.

"See you then."

"Call me if there is any change." Rush flipped the phone closed. "Shit."

Brian got out of bed and began to separate his clothing from Rush's. Rush rolled out of bed and headed to the bathroom.

"Got a mare going to foal. She's having problems," he called out.

"I got that. Can I fix you breakfast?"

"No, but some coffee to go would be great." The shower started, and as much as Brian wanted to slip under the water with Rush, he knew it'd be best if he didn't start anything.

"Sure thing." Brian hurried down the hall to the kitchen and the coffeemaker.

By the time Rush came out, dressed and drying his hair with a towel, the coffee was dripping into the pot. Brian got down a travel mug, filled it up with steaming hot black coffee, then reached into the fridge and pulled out a couple of biscuits. He popped them into the microwave to heat them up.

The buzzer went off. He pulled them out, quickly buttered them and wrapped them in a paper towel, then shoved them into Rush's hands as they walked to the door.

"It's not much, but it's better than nothing."

"Thanks, darlin'. You sure know how to treat a man to a good time."

"I had a good time, too."

Once there, Rush leaned his back against the door. "I hate for this to ruin our weekend. I'd gotten Ricky to do the chores." His face twisted in a grimace.

"Looks like we'll just have to try it again next weekend."

They kissed, careful not to crush Rush's hastily prepared breakfast between them.

"Being apart from you is killing me," Brian said, cupping Rush's face in his hand.

"Me, too. I thought we'd have more time." Rush turned slightly and laid a kiss on Brian's palm.

"It would never be enough, love."

Rush's face flushed. "I can't give you anymore, darlin'. You know that."

"I know." Brian exhaled in acceptance and stepped back.

Rush stepped through the door, trotted down the steps and got into his truck before the breath returned to Brian's lungs. With a quick wave, he was gone.

Brian leaned in the doorway long after the truck had turned the corner and disappeared. Then, he pushed off, went back inside, and crawled back into bed.

Inhaling, Brian could smell Rush's scent and the remnants of their lovemaking in his sheets. God, it was heaven. He closed his eyes and relived their time together. Each touch, each kiss, each whispered cry.

There was no way he was going to wash these sheets until next Friday.

* * *

Rush called late that evening.

"How'd it turn out?" Brian asked.

"It's a boy!" Rush sounded happy, as if he were still on a high.

"That's great. Is that what you wanted?"

"It didn't matter to me, as long as it was healthy." They both laughed.

"And is the mother okay?"

"She's fine. The vet helped her out. He had to tie a rope around the foal's leg and pull the little guy out."

Brian groaned. "Did you get there in time?"

"Yep. Saw it all, even helped with the delivery."

"Really?"

"I helped pull. Manuel kept the mama calm. Even Ricky pitched in, running to and from the vet's truck to get stuff." He chuckled.

"I'm so glad. Really. And you certainly sound like a proud papa."

"Well, he has your eyes. Big, brown, and liquid," Rush whispered.

"Now, don't you start any of that sweet talk you cowboys are so famous for." Brian laughed.

"No sweet talk?"

"No."

"How about some dirty talk?"

Brian groaned.

"I'll take that for a yes."

For the rest of the call, Rush told Brian exactly what he'd wanted to do to him the next time they were alone together. It involved whipped cream, cherries, and lots of licking.

When they hung up, Brian laid in bed making a mental shopping list for next weekend. A huge grin spread over his face.

Rush hadn't said anything about chocolate. Or bananas.

* * *

On Tuesday morning, Mrs. Waters called Brian.

"I just wanted to let you know I've made my decision."

Brian's heart pounded and he tried to keep control of his voice. "Yes, ma'am."

"Tell that young man..."

Brian waited. *Please, God, for once, do something right for Sammi.*

"Tell him I'd like to meet my grandson."

He exhaled loudly. "That's great. He'll be so happy."

"I'll leave it to you to set it up sometime this week or next."

"I will. I'll call as soon as I have a date and time, Mrs. Waters."

"That's fine, Mr. Russell. And thank you."

"Just doing my job."

"Well, some folks might have thought that meant pressuring me into seeing him instead of letting me make my own decision."

"They might."

"You're a good man, Mr. Russell."

"I try to be, Mrs. Waters."

With that, she hung up.

Brian called Sammi to tell him the news.

"I can't believe it!" Sammi shouted. "Mitchell! She's going to see me!"

Brian could hear them laughing and rejoicing in the background. He'd been forgotten for the moment, so he just sat back and listened.

A minute later, Sammi came back on. "When?"

"She left it up to you. What's your work schedule like? Can you take some time off during the day?"

"I'll ask Otis today and call you as soon as I can and set it up."

"Sounds good."

Mitchell's voice came over the line. "You're the best, Brian. I love you, man!"

More whoops and hollers and then a very full silence.

Brian closed his phone and left Sammi and Mitchell to their celebration.

Now to do something about his own life.

He straightened, brought up the Internet and then Google. Typing in Spring Lake, Texas, he hit the Go button.

The screen filled with a page of entries. He scanned them, found the one he was looking for, and clicked on it. If the mountain wouldn't come to Mohammad, maybe he should go to the mountain.

Spring Lake, Texas— Employment Opportunities

He scrolled down the list. Maintenance workers. Cafeteria workers for the high school. He grimaced. He could cook, but he looked terrible in a hair net. A librarian. Not much call for an engineer in a small town. They probably hired one on a "as needed" basis.

Some openings for accountants in the tax department. That sounded mind-numbing, but all they wanted was a four-year degree, which he had.

Bingo.

Spring Lake Police Department— An equal opportunity employer

Brian sat back and took a deep breath. He copied the Web address for inquires and then brought up his e-mail.

Composing the letter took longer than he'd thought. He kept checking their requirements to make sure he had what they needed. Then, finger poised on the mouse hovering above Send, he stopped for the first time since the crazy idea hit him and thought about what he was about to do.

Being without Rush was not an option for him. This was no way to live, and he'd decided somewhere between last weekend and this moment that he couldn't spend the rest of his life waiting on weekends.

Rush's entire life, all he was and what he knew how to be, was wrapped up in the Double T. Brian, on the other hand, had a degree that could take him just about anywhere, and he do almost anything. Law enforcement was in his blood and under his skin.

Could he really have his dream man and his dream job at the same time?

He'd never know unless he tried.

All they could do was say no thanks. It was worth a shot.

He clicked Send.

* * *

"I see on your application that you have the required law enforcement courses in addition to your degree in engineering." The chief of police looked up from the papers into Brian's face. He'd been cordial, but not overly so, but not cold. A lanky man in his fifties, he seemed to have the small-town station under control. Brian had been impressed with the efficiency of the officers who'd come and gone while he'd sat in the patrol room waiting for the chief to arrive for the interview.

"You could make a lot more money as an engineer."

"Yes. But it's always been a dream of mine to be a cop."

"You've been a PI for eight years. Licensed to carry concealed."

"Yes, sir." Brian nodded.

"Business good?"

"In Houston, yes, it's very good."

"So, why leave?" The chief looked him in the eye, searching.

"I'm tired of the big city. I'll like to try a small town." The question bordered on too personal, but to not answer might look bad or as if he had something to hide.

Whittaker didn't look like he believed it, but didn't press further. Brian had thought about what to do about being gay. Not about what to do, exactly, but what to say.

"Is there something you're not telling me?" Whittaker leaned forward, keen interest in his ice blue eyes. Brian was sure he'd used that same look with the criminals he'd come in contact with. Undoubtedly, they confessed right away, as Brian was about to do.

"Well, sir, I want to be honest with you. I don't want there to be any problems down the line because I didn't make you aware of it so I'll just get it out on the table." Brian paused, swallowed, and went for it. "I'm gay."

The chief of police blinked. Several times. Then he leaned back in his chair.

"Gay."

"I know." Brian put up his hand to stop Whittaker. "I don't look gay."

"I wasn't going to say that." He shook his head.

Now it was Brian's turn to blink. "What were you going to say?"

"That I understand. Ten years ago, times were different. Not so lenient, especially in law enforcement."

"Yes, sir." Brian nodded. "Back then, I didn't want to live a large part of my life hiding who I am. Still don't plan on living that way, even here."

"As stated on the application and the Web site, we're an equal opportunity employer, Mr. Russell." Whittaker had a funny look in his eyes as he spouted the city's diversity line. "Even out here in 'Hickland,' we have to obey the law." He gave a wry grin. "But that doesn't mean everyone will treat you with respect."

"I understand."

"Actually, you're a little older than some of our other applicants, and some of them have more training and experience."

Brian stood. He had a sinking feeling this was it, no job offer. Whittaker had come up with an excuse not to hire him because of his age.

"Where are you going?" The chief's eyebrows shot up.

"Just wanted to save you your breath turning me down. But"— he leaned on the desk between them— "I'm telling you I can do the job, sir. Whether I'm gay, or not, whether I'm older or less experienced, I can do the job. I promise you."

"It doesn't." Steepling his fingers, Whittaker leaned back in his chair.

"What?"

"I said it doesn't matter to me. I don't care what you are or aren't or how old you are. As for experience, you'd make a fine detective in a few years. What I need is a good man, someone I can trust to get the job done, to handle the citizens with an even hand and temper, and to be committed to this job."

Brian straightened.

"Sit down, son. Let's talk."

Brian sat and listened.

At the end of the interview, the two men stood, and Whittaker walked Brian to the door.

"Kristin? Please give Mr. Russell the employment package. It'll tell you everything you need to get and what we provide and all the forms you'll need to fill out about health insurance, etc. are in it. Have them completed and back to us next week. You can do your physical and drug test at that time. Report to work at the beginning of the month."

Then, he turned and held out his hand. "Welcome to Spring Lake PD, Russell."

Brian's face split into a wide grin, and he took the offered hand. "Thanks, Chief. You're not going to regret this."

"I'm sure I won't. You won't give me cause, will you?" Those icy blue eyes pinned Brian.

"No, sir." He pumped the chief's hand once more and went to the desk where Kristin was putting together the packet of papers.

"Welcome to the force, Mr. Russell." She gave him a wink and the package.

"Thanks." He nodded at her and took it, then made his escape before Chief Whittaker changed his mind.

Once in his truck, he let out a whoop of joy. He'd done it. Taken the first step to changing his life, being with the man he loved, and doing what he'd always dreamed. He tossed the package on the seat, fired up the engine, and pulled out of the lot. Taking a quick drive around town, he wanted to see what Spring Lake was all about and see if there was a real estate office. He'd have to get a house here, but he'd deal with that later.

At a gas station/convenience store, he parked and went inside for a soda and to ask for directions to the Double T. With a cold can of cola and directions in hand, he went back to his truck and got in.

Even though their date wasn't until tomorrow, he couldn't wait to see Rush and tell him the good news.

Chapter Nineteen

Rush waved and caught Manuel's eye as he came out of the barn. His foreman strolled over to the porch where Rush sat and climbed the stairs. Sliding down against the porch column, he sat, took off his hat, wiped his brow with his sleeve, and said, "Got that little colt bedded down in the new stall. He and his mom are sure happy. You've got the beginnings of a fine bloodline there, Rush."

"I know." He leaned back and placed his boots on the worn top rail.

Manual stood, holding his hand over his eyes. "Expecting visitors?"

"No." Rush shook his head.

Down the road came a dark SUV, a dust cloud following it. As soon as he recognized it, Rush felt as if a hand squeezed his heart. "Shit!" The chair fell forward, and his feet hit the ground as he stood.

Manuel glanced at him. "Recognize the truck?"

"Yeah," he muttered. What the hell was Brian doing here? Rush gave Manuel a sidelong look and wished like hell the man was somewhere else.

The vehicle stopped next to Rush's truck, and the dust settled. The door swung open, and Brian, a wide smile on his face, got out.

Rush, so mad he could spit, was down the steps and stalking toward him.

"What the hell are you doing here?" Rush bellowed. Manuel had followed and stood next to him. This was not a conversation he wanted the old man to hear.

With his eyes wide, Brian stopped, and then his eyes darted to Manuel. "I should have called. I'm sorry to have surprised you. Bad idea."

"Obviously." Rush wanted to shake Brian. What had he been thinking? As it was, he had to control himself from pulling Brian into his arms.

They stood an arm's width apart. His chest heaved with the effort to stay apart and from the rapid rise and fall of Brian's chest; it seemed he was having the same problem.

Brian looked down at the ground, seemed to gather himself and then said, "I…" His words died on his lips. He took one long look into Rush's eyes, and the heat seared Rush to the bone. Despite being furious with him, Rush recognized his hot need to pull the man to him, to kiss him, to cup his ass and grind their cocks together.

Brian shrugged and turned away. At the truck, he stopped, one hand on the open door, and opened his mouth as if to speak, then shut it. He got in, turned the truck around, and drove off.

Brian had left him. It was over.

Rush rubbed his heart and staggered. Manuel grabbed his arm and steadied him. Shit. He didn't need any help. Jerking his arm loose, he strode back to the porch, and climbed the steps. At the top, he spun around and dropped to his ass on the porch.

"Shit." He ran both hands through his hair. He'd sent Brian away, acted like the asshole he was, been rude and…a jerk. Fuck, he'd screwed the pooch for sure this time.

Manuel eased himself down next to Rush. "That the reason you been to Houston so much this month?"

Rush's head jerked up as he stared at his foreman. "What? I don't know what the fuck you're talking about." He looked down the road. The dust had settled back to the ground, and Brian's truck was long gone, taking Rush's chance for happiness with it.

"Houston. Where you've been going every couple of months for years now."

"So?"

"So, this month, you've been to Houston a couple weeks in a row. So, I figure, something's changed. And it has. You're smiling all the time, happy like I've never seen you before." Manuel's soft-spoken manner soothed Rush's rattled nerves. The old man was right on all counts.

His weathered hand rested on Rush's shoulder. "You treated him pretty rough, Rush. He didn't deserve that."

"No, he didn't," Rush whispered. He lifted his head, and he looked at Manuel.

His foreman laughed. "Son, I've known about you for ages. Since you told your daddy. He told me the same day."

"You knew?"

"That you were gay? Yes."

"But Dad…"

"Your old man was a good friend, Rush, but a shitty father. I told him so that day he beat you. He almost fired me over it." Manuel shook his head. "Things changed between us then. I continued to work for him, but our friendship had been damaged."

"You stood up for me?" Rush's eyes filled with tears. No one had ever stood up for him against his old man, not even his mother.

"Not that it did any good." He nudged Rush with his shoulder. "Seems that young man of yours is giving you a clear signal. He's standing up for you."

"Seems like it." Rush stared down the road.

"What are you willing to do for him?" Manuel gave Rush's shoulder a squeeze and stood. "Not that it means much, but I've always been proud of you, Rush."

Rush reached up and put his hand over Manuel's. "That means a lot to me."

"Now, I think you've got a phone call and some begging to do." He chuckled and walked off to the barn, leaving Rush alone.

Rush groaned. Nothing he could say was going to bring Brian back this time. It was hopeless. Manuel would know better if he'd known how many ways he'd screwed up with Brian.

Coward.

If he didn't at least try, his father had won. Even from the grave, Travis Weston had ruled his life. Now, he was letting his father destroy the one thing in the world he loved more than this stupid piece of ground.

* * *

Brian wiped his face with his sleeve and headed for the interstate.

What had he expected? Rush had told him he didn't want him to stay at the ranch, but he had no idea Rush didn't want him to even show his face. Rush's shock and embarrassment had stunned Brian.

There had been no tender gaze from him, nothing but anger and fury and outright mortification.

He'd made a terrible mistake.

Tears welled.

"I will not cry," he gritted out, but his lips quivered, on the verge of betraying him. "Not over that bastard."

He had to face the truth. From the very beginning, he'd been nothing to Rush but a booty call. A fuck buddy and phone sex and nothing more. Not even good enough to visit at his home.

What a fool he'd been, telling Rush he loved him. The cowboy probably laughed his ass off over that. Never again. He'd had it.

His phone rang. Unsnapping it from his belt, he glanced at the caller ID.

"You fucking bastard!" he yelled at the phone. The temptation to throw it out the window was powerful, but it had all his business numbers and notes on it. It'd be easier to just delete Rush's number than replace all the other stuff.

The ringing stopped. A moment later, it rolled to voice mail.

He tossed it on the seat and kept driving.

It rang again.

"Shit. Fuck. You cocksucker!" Brian shook with fury. He jerked the truck off the road and came to a stop.

Scooping up the phone, he flipped it open.

"Don't ever call me again," he shouted.

"Brian. Please. I made a terrible mistake. I panicked."

"That was panicking? You practically threw me off your ranch!"

"I know. I was just so shocked to see you."

"You used me. Again!" Brian roared into the phone.

"No! I swear. It's not like that."

Brian got out of the car and began pacing on the side of the road. "What is it like, Rush?"

"You know how I feel about you."

"Do I? Say it. Tell me like I told you."

"What?"

"Say it. Tell me how you feel about me. I've said it to you."

Silence hung in the air between them.

"Fuck you, cowboy."

"I love you." It was a whisper. A breath on the breeze. Brian almost couldn't hear it, and for a moment, he thought he'd imagined it.

"What? I want you say it out loud, and if I don't hear those words right now, I'm hanging up and it's over."

"I love you, Brian. Don't leave me."

Brian stood still, his breath in hard rasps in his chest, the phone held glued to his ear. He swallowed, licked his lips, and exhaled. He should be happy, he should be jumping up and down, or at least have a sappy grin on his face. He didn't feel happy, or much like jumping. But he did feel like a big sap. Did two out of three count?

"I can't do this, Rush. I can't keep getting hurt by you," Brian whispered.

"I'm so sorry. I know that. Please, come back. Let's talk about this. Please."

Brian lowered the phone to his side and looked up at the clouds. How many times would he go back? How much crap could he take, just to be with a man who was so buried in the closet, so deep in the dark that he couldn't see his own hand in front of his face?

"I can't live in the closet, Rush. I won't. That's not how I live my life."

"I know. We'll work something out. I swear it. Just don't leave me." Rush's angst-ridden voice choked out the words, and Brian felt the cowboy's emotions even through the tenuous cell phone connection.

Brian closed the phone and walked in a tight circle. Every cell in his body wanted Rush, but his pride kept telling him he'd be a fool to be taken in again.

He climbed back into the truck.

* * *

Rush stood in the yard in front of the house as Brian drove up. He parked, got out, but as he turned around to shut the door, Rush slammed into him and pinned him against the side of the truck.

"God, I'm so sorry, darlin'. I've been such a fool." Rush covered his face in soft kisses, roamed his hands over his chest, along his arms, and cupped his ass, pulling him in tight.

Brian brought his hands up between them, and he pushed Rush off. "Slow down. I'm here to talk, not for a booty call." His lips twisted, and his jaw worked with the strain of keeping his own hands off Rush.

Rush stepped back, hands up in surrender. "Okay. Right. Let's talk." He turned around and led the way to the porch. Brian followed. Rush stepped around a large chair and sat on a swing suspended from the porch ceiling.

"Sit with me."

Brian sat down next to Rush, and Rush put his hand on Brian's leg. It was warm, heavy, and Brian longed to feel those calloused hands on his bare skin.

Rush laughed, but it was hard and cold. "My father is rolling in his grave right about now."

"I imagine so." Brian wasn't ready to cut Rush any slack. Not yet.

Rush looked up and swallowed. Brian watched his Adam's apple bob, and focused on the spot on Rush's throat that he longed to lick. Tearing his gaze away, he fought for control and balled his hands into fists on his thighs.

"Manuel, that man who was with me when you showed up?"

"Yeah?"

"He's my foreman. He worked for my father and stayed on to work for me."

"Okay." Brian had no idea where this was going, but he wished Rush would hurry up and get there. It shouldn't feel so good to sit here with Rush.

"He knows."

"What?" Brian turned to look Rush in the eye.

"He knows about me. About us."

"Did you tell him?"

"No. He's always known I'm a faggot." Rush spit the last word out as if it tasted bad in his mouth. Personally, Brian hated that word.

"You're not a faggot, Rush. Don't ever call yourself that." He shook his head.

"Okay. He knows I'm gay. Better?"

"Yeah." Brian gave a small smile.

"My father told him all those years ago. And he kept working for me once Dad died." Rush shook his head as if he couldn't believe it.

"Well, why not?"

"I thought he was like my dad." Rush's head fell back.

"He accepts you?" Brian searched the area for the man, but he was nowhere to be seen.

"Yes. Can you believe it?"

"Yeah, I can. Not everyone your father's age is homophobic."

"I guess not." Rush sighed. "Manuel said that since I've been with you, he's never seen me happier."

"Really?"

"I've never been happier. Ever. That's God's own truth."

"I wish I could say that, Rush." Brian's voice got quiet. "But it's not been a nonstop joyride for me, cowboy."

"I know. I'm just so bad at this relationship thing. I warned you, remember?"

"Yeah, I remember. But I was so convinced I would be the one."

"You are the one, Brian."

"The one to coax you out of the closet."

Rush was silent. They sat next to each other on the swing, moving in a slow back and forth while their boot heels dragged on the wood planks of the porch. The day faded, the sky in the west a smear of crimson and orange.

Brian laid his hand on top of Rush's, and they locked fingers and continued to just swing. A man came out of the barn and up to the porch. Brian recognized him as the foreman, Manuel.

"Boss, I'm heading out. Be back in the morning, regular time." Manuel nodded to Brian. "Hello."

"Manuel, this is Brian Russell. My…" Rush stumbled.

Brian squeezed his hand. "His lover. Pleased to meet you, Manuel." He gave the man a smile and held out his hand to shake.

The older man took it. "Glad to meet you and so damn glad you came back. I hope you two work this out, but as you can see, Rush's going to need some help." Manuel chuckled. "He's a good man, Brian. You're going to have to cut him some slack."

Rush groaned. "He's done that and more, Manuel. You have no idea how patient he's been with me."

Brian shrugged. "I know a good thing when I see it."

"Well, just to let you know, he can be trained."

"Get out of here, Manuel." Rush waved him off. "You don't have to sell Brian on me."

"Well, he's doing a better job than you, cowboy." Brian laughed, finally feeling at ease again. Rush still hadn't let go of his hand.

"I guess you two have things to talk about, so I'll be going. Night, boss."

"Night, Manuel."

"Good night," Brian chimed in as the man walked off and got into a battered old truck. "He seems like a good man."

"Sure is. Best man I know. Except you." Rush brought their hands to his lips and kissed Brian's. "I don't deserve you. I know that. I just thank God you came back."

"So, let's talk." Brian wanted to tell Rush about his decision to change his life.

"Okay." They continued to swing and watch the sun set behind the low hills. Rush wrapped his arm around Brian, and Brian allowed himself to lean against the man, content to enjoy the quiet moment, looking out at the ranch, the sky, the shadows growing under the trees.

"I have to tell you something, Rush."

"You're not pregnant, are you?" Rush looked at him in mock horror.

Brian laughed. This was the Rush he loved. "No. I'm on the pill." They snorted.

"I joined the Spring Lake PD today. I report at the beginning of the month."

Chapter Twenty

Rush pulled his hand from Brian and stared at him.

"What the fuck are you talking about, Brian?" His heart thudded in his chest.

"I interviewed today with the chief. He hired me." Brian looked so happy. Rush should have been happy, but fear filled him instead.

"But, your business? Your house?" Rush stuttered.

"I have a few jobs I need to finish, but they'll be done in a week or two. I'm going to keep the house, just rent it out."

Rush didn't speak, didn't want to ask where Brian planned on living. If he moved to Spring Lake, Rush would be able to see him all the time, and that was good. They could sneak around, but eventually, people would find out they were lovers, and that was bad. Nothing stayed a secret around here for long.

Everyone would *know*.

"I'm going to find a house to rent." Brian seemed to be waiting for Rush to say something, but Rush didn't trust himself to say the right thing.

Brian stood, pulled his hand from Rush's and stared at him, waiting. Seemed not saying anything had been the wrong thing. Rush was damned if he did, damned if he didn't.

"I'll see you around." Disgusted by Rush's silence, by his refusal to come out, Brian walked to the end of the porch, then halted. What had he expected? "By the way, I told Whittaker I was gay. I wanted to be upfront about it."

Rush surged to his feet. "What the fuck? Why did you do that? Once everyone sees you with me, they'll assume I'm gay, too."

"You are gay." Brian struggled to keep his voice level. "Something you keep forgetting when it's convenient."

"I can't forget it. You keep reminding me."

"Someone has to." Brian turned away.

"Why did you have to ruin everything?" Rush yelled.

The last straw snapped, and Brian whirled around. In two strides, he was at Rush, his arm jerked back and then exploded forward, smashing into Rush's mouth. The cowboy was knocked to his ass on the porch, his lip torn and bleeding.

Brian shook his hand, the knuckles scrapped raw. "I ruined? You stupid, selfish bastard," he growled as he stood over Rush. "I offered you everything. A life, my heart, forever. And you spit on it, Rush."

Staring up at him, Rush held his hand over his mouth. Blood oozed from between Rush's fingers.

"Shit." Brian licked the back of his hand and grimaced at the metallic tang on his tongue. He'd lost control, and that had never happened to him before he'd met Rush. But the big man had pushed him, had driven him crazy, had hurt him so bad that he'd struck out. Leaving him breathless and wanting Rush. Brian's cock swelled.

What was wrong with him? He wanted to fall on top of Rush, press him into the wooden floor, crush his mouth down on Rush's swollen lips and fuck him until Rush told the world, admitted to everyone, that he was gay and Brian's lover.

"Goddamn you." Brian spun, fists still clenched, and headed down the steps. He needed to cool off, needed to get the smell of Rush's blood out of his nostrils, and get the need for Rush's body beneath his out of his blood.

Long legs striding, he followed a worn path in the low grass around the house, past the barn, and kept marching. Tears blurred his vision, but he didn't care. On autopilot, he headed as far from Rush as he could get, swallowing great gulps of air into his burning lungs.

* * *

Too stunned to move, Rush lay on the porch. He pulled his hand from his mouth and stared at it.

Blood.

Testing his lip with his tongue, he felt the cut. It was already swelling. Pushing to his feet, he steadied himself on the railing, his head still swimming from the blow.

He'd deserved that. And more.

Rush staggered into the ranch house and made his way to the kitchen. He turned on the water full blast, cupped his hands, and splashed it on this face, washing the blood away.

Then he got ice from the freezer and wrapped it in a towel. He slumped into a kitchen chair, held the ice pack to his mouth, leaned his head back, and closed his eyes.

He had no idea how long he'd sat there, not thinking, wallowing in the pain of his busted lip and his shattered life.

"What the hell happened to you?"

He cracked open one eye. Manuel stood with his hands on his hips, head cocked like a feisty gray-haired rooster.

"It didn't go like I planned."

"No shit." Manuel pulled out a chair and sat at the table. "Where's Brian?"

Rush shrugged. "Gone."

"His truck is still outside."

"I didn't see. I was lying on my ass, looking up at the stars circling the porch ceiling at the time."

"Undoubtedly deserved."

"What are you doing back here?"

"Forgot my list for the feed supplies." He held up a piece of paper.

Rush sighed. "I've really fucked this up, Manuel."

"Fucking is easy, Rush. Relationships are hard. Don't guess you've had much practice with those." Manuel stared at him, his gaze boring into Rush's heart.

"Yeah, I've got the fucking down. And I'm a master at the fucking up part." He tried to laugh, but it pulled at his lip, so he replaced the ice pack.

Manuel looked out the window. "It's dark. Any idea where he might have gone?"

“No.” Rush stood, staring out through the panes of glass. “He could be anywhere.”

“We’ll give him another thirty minutes or so; then we’d better go look for him.”

“You go on home. I’ll find him. Apologize, grovel…” Rush muttered. “I seem to be doing a lot of that lately.”

Manuel slapped him on the back. “You’ll get it right. If not this time, the next.”

Rush shook his head. “There’ll never be a next time. Brian was it. The one.”

Without replying, Manuel left Rush alone in the kitchen, staring out at the dark.

* * *

Brian swore and kicked another rock, sending it flying into the night. Each one was a tiny Rush being kicked out of Brian’s life with the pointed end of his boots. He’d been walking for a while, each step taking him farther and farther from Rush, and that was just peachy damn keen with him.

The rock vanished into the blackness around him. The ping as it landed broke the night noises. It tumbled along the ground and then was silent. He stopped and looked around.

Where the hell was he? The sky was moonless and the stars weren’t out yet. How did it get so dark so fast? Must be the country. No lights from the city, nor from the highway. No lights at all.

He turned in a slow circle. Not even lights from the ranch house.

Great. Just fucking great. He was lost.

If he just followed the path back, he'd be fine. If he could see it. Squinting in the darkness, he strained to find some outline of the worn path he'd followed.

He couldn't just stand here all night.

Brian started walking back in the direction he'd figured he'd come from. Fifteen minutes later, he was still surrounded by the night.

"Fuck!" This wasn't cool. He could barely see his way now.

He didn't let a little thing like darkness bother him; he just kept going, marching as if he'd had orders from military command. March or die.

He stumbled, losing his footing on a scattering of loose rocks. Arms flailing as he twisted, he went down on one knee, and pain shot up his leg. With a useless attempt at righting himself, he went down on his side in the dirt.

The ground beneath him was cold, hard, and unyielding. Above, the sky was so dark he couldn't tell if he was floating or not.

The pain in his knee throbbed, and he tried to straighten it. He kicked a large rock with his heel, and it shifted out of the way.

There are some sounds he'd recognize in a heartbeat. His lover's voice. The cocking of a pistol. The warning rattle of a snake.

It filled the night, like someone's radio turned up too loud, and his heart was the pounding bass. Warmth drained from Brian's body, disappearing as if it had been sucked out of him. All that was left was cold terror.

The rattle lessened.

Brian took a tentative breath.

Silence.

He drew his good leg up and angry rattling broke the night.

He froze. The rattling stopped.

His dream came back to him. The terror, the night sky, the inability to move.

All that was missing was Rush trying to kill him.

And he'd given Rush the motive when he'd punched him.

Brian closed his eyes, got control of his runaway heart and his imagination. He swallowed, but there wasn't enough moisture left in his mouth.

He tried to move his other leg, but the pain wasn't going to allow it. Even the small movement set off the rattler. He stilled.

How long could he lie here with a snake curled up next to him?

Maybe it would move off. Get hungry and leave. Chase down some poor field mouse or a lizard. It couldn't be interested in him, could it?

The adrenaline surged, and he fought the impulse to jump up, run, and never look back. His muscles tightened, ready to take flight.

No fucking way. He didn't even know where it actually was hiding. Bringing his urge to run under control, he held still.

Somewhere near his feet was a snake. Left or right?

He raised his arm on the right, and the rattler sounded.

Okay. Right side— check.

He inched his arm back down without setting off the snake.

If he just kept still, he'd be fine. The ground grew colder, and a shiver ran through his body. How cold did it get out here at night? Couldn't be any colder than in the city.

Sixties, tops.

Now all he had to do was wait until Rush showed up and shot him.

* * *

Rush stood on the porch and stared into the night. He switched to night vision and scanned the area around the ranch.

He cupped his hands around his mouth and called, "Brian!"

No answer, not even the dogs. Where were the dogs? Probably off chasing possums and raccoons in one of the outer pastures.

Thirty minutes had come and gone.

He stepped off the porch onto the steps.

In the distance, a series of howls broke the night.

Coyotes.

Rush turned around, went inside to the gun rack, and took down his rifle.

* * *

No fucking way. Coyotes? Brian groaned.

This was too much. Really. Like some bad B movie with that second-rate action hero, Bruce somebody.

Brian laughed.

The snake rattled.

The coyotes joined in.

Are we having fun yet?

He'd take Rush with the rifle right about now.

* * *

Rush followed the tracks of Brian's boots past the barn. They came and went as the ground hardened into packed earth and mixed with the prints of hooves and paws. Rifle slung over his shoulder, he looked up, scanned the night, and kept going.

The coyotes sounded like they were hunting. A small pack, maybe five or six. They could bring down a stray calf, or a sick steer, but a man?

If he were on the ground. Injured. Unconscious.

Rush picked up his pace, broke into a trot, his long legs ate up the distance. Breathless, he paused at the top of a rise and looked down into the wash. On his left in the distance, the coyotes were gathered, yipping and working up their courage.

There on the ground lay a body. With his heart in his throat, he slid down the slope, reached the bottom, and stalked forward.

"Brian?"

"Rush?" Brian squinted in the dark, but all he could see was a tall dark shape moving towards him.

It had to be Rush. Unarmed. He let out a sigh. "Wait, don't come closer. There's a snake somewhere next to me. It's too dark for me to see it. On the right. A rattler."

Rush froze. With a quick movement, he swung what could only be a rifle off his shoulder, leveled it at waist height, and pointed it at Brian.

Brian's heart stopped. This was it. His premonition come true.

Rush was going to kill him.

"Don't move."

"Rush. Don't do this. I'm sorry. Really. You don't have to do this." Brian held out his hand to ward off Rush and the snake's death song filled the air.

"Don't fucking move," Rush growled.

"Rush. Don't. Please," Brian's voice cracked as he begged for his life.

"Trust me."

"What?"

"Just for once, trust me." Rush brought the rifle to his shoulder. His actions calm, sure, steady.

Trust this man, let go of his fear. Of his vision. Brian closed his eyes, took a deep breath, and nodded once. "Okay." He held still and waited for the shot.

The crack of the shot exploded, and the muzzle flare blinded Brian. The ground near his calf shook. The snake blew into the air and landed across his legs in a tangle of thick, heavy loops.

Brian screamed.

Rush dropped the rifle, ran to Brian, grabbed the snake, and tossed it into the night.

"You're all right, darlin'," Rush crooned as he gathered Brian into his arms.

"How did you… It's pitch dark." Brian was so cold, and he couldn't control the shaking that racked his body.

"You're not the only one with powers." Rush pulled Brian to his feet and let him rest his weight on his shoulder. "I can see in the dark."

Brian shifted his grip around Rush's waist. "You could have told me."

"I was going to." They began hobbling back to the house.

"So that's how you saw me behind the dumpster. And in my garden."

"Yep."

"Why didn't you tell me? Especially after I told you about my abilities. I trusted you, but you couldn't trust me." Brian didn't want to admit how much that hurt him.

"I was afraid."

"You're an asshole, Weston," Brian muttered.

"Yep."

They were silent the rest of the way, until they reached the front of the house.

Brian broke from Rush, limping on one leg. "I'm going home, Rush. I have a long drive."

"You're leaving?" Rush leaned the rifle against the porch wall.

"Yeah. Like I said, it's a long drive back."

"You could stay here tonight." Rush looked at him.

"What would the neighbors say?" Brian shook his head. "I promised you I wouldn't out you. I'm not going to do it. It's your decision."

"Brian..." Rush reached for him, but Brian took two halting steps back.

"I've got to go. Thank you for saving my life, cowboy." He turned and limped over to the truck, opened the door, and slid inside.

The door closed, and he hit the ignition. The Tahoe roared to life as he hit his lights, illuminating Rush. The cowboy looked done in. His lip was about two sizes bigger, and there was a dark spot, probably a bruise, on his chin.

Brian put the Tahoe into gear, backed out, and headed down the road.

He looked over his shoulder. Rush stood in the yard, hands in the pockets of his jeans, watching him leave. For a split second, Brian thought he might run after him, call out, wave, something to signal Brian to come back. That he was ready.

That he loved Brian enough.

He turned back to navigate the dark road.

He flicked his eyes to the rearview mirror for one last look.

Rush climbed the steps of the porch and broke Brian's heart.

Chapter Twenty-one

"I'm so nervous, Mitch. What if she doesn't like me?" Sammi twisted his fingers as he, Mitchell, and Brian walked up the sidewalk to his grandmother's house. This was what he'd wanted ever since he'd learned he might have a chance to find his family, but now that he was here, he was terrified.

"Don't worry, babe. She doesn't have to love you, just meet you. And you don't have to love her either." Mitchell's words reassured him, but it was Mitchell's feelings of well-being and calm washing over him that really helped settle his nerves.

Brian rang the bell. The door opened and Mrs. Waters stood there. His grandmother. His mother's mother.

Everyone stared at each other. Mitchell stepped back, leaving Brian and Sammi on the front line. Sammi felt exposed, vulnerable as he observed her. Small, like him, she peered back at him with the same dark eyes as his.

He searched for her in the jumble of Brian and Mitchell's thoughts. Brian worried that this had been a mistake. Mitchell hoped he wouldn't be too hurt if she rejected him.

None of that mattered. He had *family*. Whether she wanted him of not, he belonged.

“Mrs. Rose Waters, this is Samuel Waters, your grandson.” Brian motioned to Sammi.

“Hello.” Sammi flashed a nervous smile. “Grandmother.” He gave his bangs a flick of his hand to push them out of the way.

“Come on in.” She stepped aside and they entered. After shutting the door, she led them to the living room and pointed to the couch and chairs. Sammi sat on the couch, and Mitchell and Brian sat on chairs.

Mrs. Waters sat on the couch with her grandson.

“And who are you?” She looked at Mitchell.

“I’m Sammi’s friend. I’m here for moral support.” He gave her a smile but her mouth was a thin, tight line.

Sammi felt her uneasiness with the meeting. Unhappy, and quite unsettled. Not a good beginning, but he’d work hard to prove himself to her. He could be a good grandson if she’d just give him a shot.

She stared at him, then spoke, “So, Samuel, what do you want to know?” She sat back, hands folded neatly in her lap.

Sammi opened his mouth, then frowned. “Why you don’t like me.”

She gasped.

“Oh, I look too much like my mother. I’m sorry. I didn’t mean to hurt you.” He reached out to her and placed his hand over hers.

She jerked away, her eyes wide.

“Sammi can hear the thoughts of others, remember?” Brian jumped in. “I know it’s a little disconcerting, but…”

"It's all right." She waved her hand to dismiss his words. "Lydia was just like him." She stared into his eyes. "You look just like her, Samuel."

Sammi smiled. "Thank you. Did she look like you or her father?"

"Like me. But she had her father's willfulness." She chuckled.

"Mitchell says I'm determined."

"And stubborn," Mitchell added.

"Do you remember your mother, Samuel?"

"Call me Sammi. With an *i*."

"All right."

"No, I was very young when she left…" He stopped. "When she put me up for adoption."

"Where are my manners?" Rose stood, went into the kitchen, and returned with a tray holding a pitcher of iced tea and four glasses. "Help yourselves. I'll be right back."

The guys looked at each other, shrugged, and Mitchell poured out the tea.

Rose returned, carrying a small box. She sat down and took the lid off it.

"These are some of your mother's things, Sammi. I kept them hidden from her father. He would have thrown them out."

Sammi's heart was a staccato beat in his chest. His mother's things. Never in his dreams did he ever think he'd get to see, much less touch, something that had belonged to her.

She dug in the box, pulled out a few pieces of baby clothing, a well-loved doll, and a small photo album. “Here. You should have this, I think.”

She handed it to Sammi, and he took it with trembling hands. He placed it in his lap and opened it. As he turned the pages, taking in each photo, memorizing the face of a beautiful young girl who had never grown up, his eyes filled with tears.

“She’s so beautiful.” He blinked, and the tears ran down his cheeks.

“You look just like her, Sammi.” Rose leaned close and ran her finger over the image. “Same small build, same dark hair and eyes.”

“Your hair and eyes.” Sammi glanced up at her as a wave of longing and sadness poured off her. “Don’t cry.” He reached up and wiped a tear from her cheek.

“You’re a great one to tell a body not to cry.” She returned the favor.

Sammi shrugged. “You know, it doesn’t mean you’re weak if you cry. It means you have a loving heart, strong feelings, and a good soul. I can tell that about a person, you know.”

She smiled at him. “Just like Lydia.”

Sammi gasped as a window to her feelings opened. She loved him, and she didn’t even know about him, what he’d done, or how low he’d sunk.

“I’ve had a troubled life, too,” he whispered.

“Do you want to tell me about it?” She placed her hand on his and gave it a squeeze.

"Yes, I do. But I'm afraid once you hear about it you won't want me." He searched her eyes, but she gave him another squeeze.

"I want you. No matter what you've done, Sammi. Besides, I can tell you're a good man."

"You can?" Sammi straightened.

"I may not be as in tune as your mother or you, but I've always been a good judge of people." She winked at Brian. "Never would have let you in if I wasn't."

"Well, I'll be," Brian muttered.

Mitchell caught Brian's eye and jerked his head toward the kitchen. The men rose and gave Sammi and his grandmother space and privacy.

Sammi sent Mitchell his love and sent Brian his thanks.

Without these two incredible men in his life, he would still be a sex slave, a prisoner, unloved, without friends or family.

"Do you think my mother loved me?" Sammi stared into his grandmother's dark eyes.

"I'm sure of it." She smiled at him, then turned the page and told him about the next picture in the little album.

* * *

Moving day. Brian drove the van with Mitchell and Sammi following in the Tahoe. They pulled up to the small house he'd rented in Spring Lake. It was simple, but all he needed. Two bedrooms, living area, one bathroom, kitchen, a laundry room, and a carport for his SUV.

More than enough for a man living alone.

He backed the truck into the drive, parked, and got out.

"Wasn't your rental agent supposed to be here?" Mitchell asked as he met Brian on the front sidewalk.

"Yeah. I'll call her. She's probably running late." Brian flipped open his phone, searched his contacts, and hit the number.

"Spring Lake Reality," a chipper voice answered.

"This is Brian Russell. I'm at the house and need the keys."

"Mr. Russell? What house?"

"The house I rented last week. Put down the eight-hundred-dollar deposit for." Brian was getting irritated.

"I'm sorry. Hold on. Let me get someone to help you." She put him on hold and country music came on.

"What's going on?" Mitchell asked. Sammi waited next to him, his eyes darting from Brian to Mitchell to the house.

"There's a problem with the house." Brian shrugged.

"That's okay. We've got all day to unpack." Mitchell pulled Sammi to him and tucked the smaller man under his arm.

"Don't worry Brian. It'll be all right." Sammi grinned up at him from under that sexy mop of black bangs.

"Not worried. Not yet."

The phone line clicked. "Mr. Russell. It's Mrs. Hardt. I'm sorry, but Mr. Weston came by my office this week and cancelled your lease. He said you'd found something else, and he was handling it for you."

"What?" Brian yelped.

"Was that wrong? Mr. Weston said he knew you and I had no reason not to believe him. He's an upstanding member of this community. Been here all his life."

"Fine. Never mind. I'll get this straightened out with him and get back to you."

Brian snapped his phone shut. "That son of a bitch."

"What's going on?" Mitchell's brow furrowed.

"Rush. He cancelled my lease," Brian growled.

"He can't do that, can he?" Sammi asked.

"Seems so. Seems he's a respected member of this fair city, and people will do whatever he says." Brian cursed and kicked the nearest tire of the truck.

He circled around and flipped open his phone. "We'll just see about that. I have to report to work in the morning, house, or no house, and he can't stop me from doing that."

"Are you sure?" Sammi's question froze Brian.

"Just how much pull does this guy have, Brian?" Mitchell chimed in.

"Not enough, I hope. If he thinks he can run me off this easily, he's mistaken."

He punched up the police department's number. "This is Brian Russell. Is the chief in?"

"Hold on, Brian, I'll see." The dispatcher put him on hold.

"Chief Whittaker. What's up, Russell?"

"I've got a problem. There's been a mix up with my lease. I've got to find a place to stay tonight, but I'm going to be there in the morning."

"Hmm. Where are you?"

Brian gave him the address.

"Okay, I'll expect you in." The chief hung up.

"Next up. The cowboy." Brian grimaced as he punched up the contact list.

A black Ford F-250 pulled up behind the van.

"He's here," Sammi said.

Brian turned around and watched Rush slid out of the truck, shut the door, and walk toward him.

"You've got some nerve, you bastard." Fists raised and ready to do battle, Brian advanced. He'd taken the big man down once; he'd do it again if he had to.

"Wait a second. Hold on." Rush's hands went up in surrender.

"You cancelled my rental. That was low, cowboy. But it won't matter. I'll just get a motel room until I get this straightened out."

"I need to explain. Can you just listen to me?"

"Listen to you!" Brian surged forward, and Mitchell caught him, pulling him back.

A police cruiser slid to a stop, and Chief Whittaker got out.

"What's going on here?" He looked all business in his khaki shirt, black pants, and spit shined black boots. Pushing his Stetson back from his forehead, he scanned the two men. "Russell, explain."

"*Mr. Weston* cancelled my rental agreement without my authorization."

Whittaker leveled his no-nonsense gaze at Rush. "Rush, is that right?"

Rush looked at Brian being restrained by Mitchell, and his heart bled. He'd wanted to do this, but the growing crowd was daunting, to say the least.

Whittaker stared at him, waiting for an answer.

Brian's eyes burned in undisguised anger, and in that instant, Rush feared that whatever he said would be wasted breath.

"Rush, what's going on here?" Whittaker's gaze shot from Brian to Rush. "I can see that you two know each other."

No going back. He'd do what he came here to do, damn the consequences.

Rush took a deep breath, gathered that famous Weston courage, and looked into Brian's eyes. "He doesn't need the house. I want him to move in with me and live at the Double T."

Whittaker straightened, pushed his hat back even higher, and narrowed his eyes. "Now, why would he want to do that?"

Rush kept his gaze locked with Brian's. "He's my lover."

One eyebrow rose. "Well." He paused. "Russell? Is this true?"

"Are you serious?" Brian asked Rush, ignoring the chief's questions.

"As a snake. A rattler, actually." Rush gave him a soft smile as Brian's searching gaze plumbed his heart. "I know I've screwed things up between us. Maybe for good. But if there's even a chance, I still want you. If you'll have me."

Mitchell and Sammi moved quietly away to the Tahoe.

Brian stared at him. "I don't believe it." He shook his head.

Whittaker cleared his throat. "Rush, you know what you're saying, don't you?"

"That I'm gay." Rush nodded. "And that I'm in love with Brian."

"Just checkin'." He turned at faced Brian. "No matter where you wind up living, I'll see you at seven a.m. sharp at the station."

"Yes, sir." Brian nodded, his gaze not leaving Rush's face.

The chief got back in his patrol car and left.

Mitchell and Sammi leaned against the Tahoe, arms wrapped around each other.

"Well, Brian. Where should we go?" Mitchell asked. "To the motel or to the ranch?"

Brian walked up to Rush, stood toe-to-toe with him and locked eyes. "You did it."

"Yeah. After you left, I had to face facts. If I wanted you, I had to accept myself."

"And you don't care who knows?"

"Not really." He sighed and cupped Brian's face. "All this time I thought I'd been ashamed of who I am, but what I was really ashamed of was my cowardice. Not standing up to my father, or to this town. But once I admitted that there was nothing wrong with how I feel about you, and about myself, it was an easy choice to make." He exhaled. "It's so freeing. I never thought it would feel like this."

"You're not afraid of what the people here in Spring Lake might think of you?"

"Yeah, I am. I won't lie to you. Losing you terrified me more." Rush's smile flashed, and then he sobered. "Forgive me. Let me make it up to you, every day of our lives, darlin'. Let's live together at the ranch until we're both old, and all we can do is sit on that porch swing and watch the sunsets."

Brian rested his face in Rush's calloused hand and closed his eyes.

This was what he'd dreamed of since he'd met Rush in that dark alley. He opened his eyes and looked into Rush's brilliant blue eyes. God, he loved this man, despite all of Rush's screwed-up, fumbling attempts at finding and accepting love. It would be hard, no doubt about that. Rush was going to be a handful, but Brian could handle the big cowboy.

"Mitchell? Sammi?" Brian called.

"Yes?" They stepped forward, all eyes on him.

"Follow us to the Double T. After we unload my stuff, we can come back into town and have dinner."

"Sounds like a plan," Mitchell replied.

Rush exhaled and pulled Brian against him.

"Careful, cowboy. Someone might see us," Brian warned.

"Let 'em look, I don't care." He planted a kiss on Brian's lips. Brian's arms slipped around his shoulders as he melted into Rush.

"Hey, guys," Mitchell called. "Get a room."

The two men broke apart. Rush slung his arm around Brian's shoulder and grinned at Mitchell and Sammi.

"Let's get going. I have to get a good night's sleep tonight." Brian headed to the truck.

Rush groaned. "I guess that means you'll have to take the guest room tonight, because if I get my hands on you, there will not be a moment of sleep to be had." He grinned wickedly and climbed into the driver's seat of his Ford.

They pulled out, followed by Mitchell and Sammi in the Tahoe, and headed to the Double T ranch.

Chapter Twenty-two

“That’s the last of the boxes.” Brian fell into the chair in the kitchen and took the cold beer Mitchell handed him.

“How can one man generate so much stuff?” Mitchell asked. “I never realized you were such a pack rat.” He grinned as he took a sip from his bottle.

“I’m not a pack rat. There are important documents in those boxes.”

“You should have them scanned to disk, then have them destroyed. There are companies that do that, you know.” Mitchell laughed.

“Destroy them?” Brian’s eyebrows shot up.

“Hey, I don’t mind, darlin’. I’ve got lots of space to store them.” Rush came to Brian’s rescue as he slid into a seat and placed a possessive hand on Brian’s shoulder.

“Thanks.” Brian held up his beer and the two men clinked bottles.

Sammi sat next to Mitchell and whispered in his ear. Mitchell nodded.

“What’s up, you two?” Brian asked.

Sammi looked at Mitchell in question. Mitchell said, “Go ahead, babe. Tell them.”

"I want to thank you, Brian, for finding my family."

"No thanks needed. You paid your bill. We're square." Brian waved him away.

"This isn't money." Sammi licked his lips. "I want to give you something that means a lot more than money."

Brian sat up. "What's that? 'Cause the money is pretty good, I have to tell you."

"I want you to experience what I have with Mitchell." He gave them a tentative smile and a toss of his bangs.

"What's he talking about?" Rush looked at Brian.

Brian stared at Sammi. "He's talking about the way they can hear each other's thoughts, feel each other."

Sammi grinned. "That's right."

"Can you do it?" Mitchell asked him.

"I'm not positive, but I think, if I link them through me, I can." Sammi nodded. "That is, if they want to."

Brian looked at Rush. He could see the disbelief in his cowboy's eyes. "I know you're not sure about this, but I'd like to try it."

Rush looked at Sammi, then Mitchell. "Can you really…"

"The sex is phenomenal." Mitchell grinned at him. "Trust me. You want to do this."

Rush shrugged. "I'm game."

"Great! Now all we need is a big bed and to get naked," Sammi quipped.

Brian choked, and Rush sprayed his beer across the table.

"You're pulling my chain, right, Sammi?" Brian sputtered.

"No. We could do it right here, but I think once you connect, you're going to want to be naked, very quickly." He gave Rush a sexy slow smile as his eyebrows rose.

The men looked at each other.

"What do you think, Mitchell? What kind of involvement between Sammi and us will there be?" Brian asked.

"From what Sammi has told me, he'll start by simply touching you both, skin to skin."

"Where you want the touch to be is up to you," Sammi added.

Rush shifted in his chair. "What about you, Mitchell? Are you just going to hang around out here?"

"If you're asking me to join you, I'd love to. If you want to be alone, that's okay, too." Mitchell shrugged.

Across the table, he locked eyes with Brian. Brian turned to Rush. "What do you want? Your call. I know you've got concerns with Mitchell and me, and I don't want to cause any problems between us."

Sammi leaned forward. "How about this? Let's set some rules. I have to touch you both, so your emotions and sexual feelings can flow back and forth through me, but I'll only touch you where you want me to, nowhere else. If anything more evolves between us everyone must agree, but let's agree that when we finish, it's with our own partner."

"Okay." Rush nodded. "We can dance with each other as the mood takes us, but we end with the one who brought us."

"I agree," Brian said. "How about you, Mitchell?"

"I'm in." He raised his beer bottle and the men toasted their agreement.

"So, where's the bed?" Sammi stood.

Rush opened the door to his bedroom and led them inside. A king-size four poster bed stood against the far wall between two windows. A quilt, obviously handmade, covered the bed, and four large pillows in plain white cases leaned against the dark wood headboard. On either side was a nightstand.

"Now what?" he asked.

"We get naked." Sammi began to undress. Mitchell stepped up to him and took over unbuttoning his shirt. As Brian watched, the two men began kissing, their hands working off their clothing.

He turned to Rush. "Come here, cowboy."

Rush glanced at Brian. "I've never done this before. In front of someone."

"Me either. It's kind of wild, huh?" He pulled Rush to him, and they kissed.

In a few minutes, there were four incredible, naked male bodies adorning the room. Sammi led Mitchell to the bed.

"Rush and Brian, you two get in the bed. Leave enough space between you for me," Sammi instructed.

They climbed on top of the quilt and stretched out on their backs.

"There's lube in the desk. Do you need a condom?" Rush asked.

Sammi shook his head. "No, we're both clean."

"So are we." Brian took Rush's hand and brought it to his lips.

Sammi got on the bed and positioned himself between the men, near their feet.

"Mitch, get behind me."

Mitchell climbed up and sat behind Sammi, with his hands on his young lover's shoulders.

"Now, I'm going to touch your legs first. Try to make contact with each of you." Sammi reached out his hands and stroked them.

Brian shivered as Sammi's soft fingers glided over his leg from just below his knee to the top of his foot. Sammi repeated it, and each time, Brian felt more pressure, more of a tingle.

He glanced over at Rush. His eyes were closed, and a hint of a smile played on his lips. Brian reached out, took Rush's hand, and they clasped fingers. The tingling increased.

He looked at Sammi. Mitchell's arms wrapped around the smaller man's chest, his fingers teased Sammi's small, dark nipples. Sammi's head fell back, and his eyes closed as Mitchell laved his throat.

Jesus, they were beautiful. Brian's cock began to fill as he watched. His grip on Rush tightened, and he broke his gaze away from the men in front of him and looked at his lover. His blue eyes were as dark as storm clouds, and he rolled onto his side and pulled Brian to him.

His cock was erect, jutting into the space between them.

"Can you hear me?"

Brian startled at the voice in his head, and his gaze jerked to Sammi. The younger man watched him with a half smile. Brian nodded.

"Can you hear me?"

Rush gasped and looked up at Sammi kneeling between their bodies.

"Shit," he whispered.

"Didn't really believe, did you?"

Sammi gave a soft chuckle, and then, as Mitchell bit his neck, he arched his body up and moaned. A jerk of sexual energy shot up Rush's leg and stiffened his cock.

He watched, fascinated, as Mitchell's hand began a slow slide down Sammi's chest, and he took the guy's sweet cock in his grip. With a few slow strokes, Sammi's dick was hard and full, its tip flushed, but Sammi's hands continued to touch their legs.

It made him so fucking horny. Made his mouth water for lack of a dick to suck. He glanced at Brian. He was staring back at him. Brian reached out and stroked his chest, his fingernail scraping over his taut nipple. Rush groaned.

"Can you hear each other?"

Both men shook their heads as their hands caressed each other. He'd have to increase his influence on them. They could each hear him, but that's where it ended.

"Mitchell," he whispered. "They can't hear each other. I need to..."

"Do it, babe. Whatever it takes." Mitchell stroked him, his powerful grip slid up and then down his cock. Sammi shuddered.

Rush and Brian, their dicks erect and straining away from their bodies, touched each other.

"Get closer."

The men moved together. Cocks touched and danced in the air. Sammi slid his hands up their legs and leaned forward until he was within reach of their thick erections.

He took one in each hand. Heated flesh filled his palm.

"Shit." Rush groaned as Brian whimpered.

Sammi brought them together, clasped his hands around their shafts, and stroked them. He opened himself to them and shuddered as their arousals washed over him. Their cocks jerked in his hand as he concentrated on sharing it with them.

Feeding it back, he let their sexual energies flow through him and over each other.

"Oh, goddamn," Brian cried out.

It was working.

Rush sucked in a breath, shuddered, and surged forward. Sammi was hit with Rush's ramped-up sexual energy, and his own prick stiffened in Mitchell's hand. He let some of the energy leak to Mitchell, and his lover bit down on his shoulder.

Mitchell's hand crept around to his ass, cupping and pinching his globes, then slipped his finger into Sammi's crevasse.

"I need lube, babe."

"Rush, give me some lube," Mitchell said.

Rush reached around, jerked open the drawer, grabbed the tube, and tossed it onto the bed at Sammi's knees. Mitchell picked it up, and it disappeared from his sight. A moment later, Mitchell's lubed finger circled his hole.

"Oh, yes, Mitch," he breathed and sent his lover his feelings. Mitchell moaned against his ear, his tongue flicking into the shell.

Rush and Brian's hips thrust together, urging Sammi to work their dicks harder, their precum lubricating his fists.

"Oh God, someone suck me!" Rush cried out.

"Do it, babe," Mitchell whispered.

"Can I do it, Brian?"

"Yeah, I want to watch," Brian rasped.

Sammi pulled Rush's prick up, leaned down, and laved the head with his tongue. As Rush moaned, he reached for Brian and pulled him into a hard, needy kiss. Sammi watched the men, their mouths open, tongues thrusting into the warm caverns, their bodies connecting at their chests, but still leaving room for him. Then, they broke the kiss and turned to watch him.

Sammi dipped down and took Rush in his mouth and swallowed him. He tasted different from Mitchell, but familiar. He inhaled Rush's scent and rubbed his nose in the tight curls at the base of Rush's cock.

As Sammi leaned over to take Rush's dick, he presented his beautiful ass to Mitchell. Mitchell spread the cheeks apart to glimpse Sammi's pink rose. He ran his lubed finger around it, circling it until it pursed its outer edge at him.

He slipped his finger in and Sammi grunted, pushed back into his hand, and sent his feelings out.

Both Rush and Brian moaned. He shuddered.

Twisting his finger, he found Sammi's sweet spot, massaged it, and kept his grip on his lover's shaft. Sammi's body shook and his arousal flooded Mitchell.

Mitchell's cock stood straight up, and he rubbed it against Sammi's butt cheek, but watched the two men over Sammi's back.

Clutching at each other, they writhed on the bed as Sammi worked his magic on Rush's dick and sent everyone the combined pleasure that coursed through him.

Sammi was good at head, for damn sure. He'd been sucked off by many men, but they'd paled to Brian. Now, Sammi came in a close second.

It amazed him. How he could feel all their pleasures, all their arousals, all their heat. Mind-blowing sex. The erotic amplitude was off the charts, flooding his erogenous zones and making his skin so sensitive it hurt, but fuck, it hurt so good that he wanted more.

"Brian?"

More than anything, he wanted to meet Brian in this place, to feel how Brian felt when he made love to him. To share how he felt with Brian. To let him feel all the love he didn't have words for.

There was no answer.

"I can't hear Brian."

Chapter Twenty-three

"Okay, Rush."

He'd have to do something. They were all jumbled. Sammi thought hard about how to separate each of them out. Could he do it?

"Mitchell, back off."

Mitchell's touch lessened, his finger pulled out, and Sammi let his contact with his lover slip away.

"Take care of them."

Mitchell sat back but kept a light hand on the small of Sammi's back and sent his reassurance to Sammi.

Brian groaned. God, this was heaven. He'd never felt so *much* before. So incredibly turned on, so hot, so needing to be fucking Rush. The touch of the cowboy's hands weren't enough.

"I need Rush."

"Soon."

The energy lessened. Instinctually, Brian knew that one of them had left, or been pulled away. He glanced up at Sammi, bent over Rush's cock and laving it with the flat of his tongue while fingering Rush's balls.

Mitchell sat back behind him, his dark eyes watching his lover tease Rush's cock.

Sammi gave Rush's engorged cock a last lick, then straightened.

Another lessening of the sexual energy that warped through Brian's body, a soft echoing of Sammi's arousal fading in the mix of panting, grunting, glorious sex.

"Rush?"

"Brian. Oh, God, Brian, it's you."

Sammi's presence fell away.

All Rush knew was Brian. Without thinking, he surged toward Brian, and pulled him in tight. Brian's firm body was hot, rigid all down the long length of him. Brian's sexual arousal ramped up, his need, and his hunger flooded Rush.

Their cocks scraped, pressed into their bellies. He wrapped his leg around Brian's calf, holding him in place as he pulled Brian on top of him. He cupped Brian's ass and ground his hips against his body.

Sweet Jesus, Brian loved him. It emanated from Brian in waves, like heat on asphalt and shook him to his core. Brian had said the words and he'd believed them, but to actually feel it made his love more real, more tangible.

It touched somewhere dark and hidden inside him and illuminated every corner of his soul.

"It's so good. Sweet Jesus, Brian." He gasped. "It's so good."

Rush's heightened arousal ripped through Brian, and he cried out his love's name.

He captured Rush's face in his hands, and crushed his mouth down on the cowboy. He wanted to be inside Rush, so deep he couldn't find his way out. In the far reaches of his mind, Sammi lingered, and kept the connection between him and Rush alive.

"Thank you for this, Sammi."

"I love you, Rush."

"I love you, Brian."

Breaking contact with the lovers on the bed, Mitchell slipped off the bed and pulled Sammi with him. For a moment, they held each other and watched as Brian and Rush came together.

"Damn, they're so beautiful." Mitchell's hands feathered across Sammi's chest and down to cup his balls.

"Turns you on, huh?"

"Fuck, yes." He laved Sammi's shoulder.

"We should leave them alone."

"Not yet." His lips moved against the nape of Sammi's neck as he sent the image of Brian and Rush fucking to his lover.

"You're a bad boy, Mitch. You need to be punished."

Mitchell groaned. *"Will you punish me?"*

Sammi turned to him, wrapped his arms around Mitchell's neck and his legs around Mitchell's waist, and kissed him.

"Yes, I will."

He rubbed his cock up and down Mitchell's belly as the bigger man supported him with strong arms. Mitchell cupped his ass and pulled him tight, capturing his cock between their bodies.

"Make me hurt, babe."

"I know what you want."

He climbed down, took Mitchell's hand, and led him out of the bedroom to finish their lovemaking alone.

Rush found the lube and pressed it into Brian's hand. "Get me ready. Now." He spread his legs wide.

Brian nodded, covered his fingers with the sticky goo, reached down between Rush's legs, and spread it in the crack of Rush's ass. Rush's hunger flooded him as he stroked the sensitive skin between Rush's balls and his backdoor.

Sammi had left them, but their connection held strong. He wondered how much longer it would last. Not long, he'd bet.

The need to get inside Rush, couple with him, surged, and the fear of losing this moment and this sharing left him shivering with need.

He dragged Rush's ass toward him, pushed his knees down and apart and leaned in, skewering his lover on his aching dick.

Rush's ecstasy at being taken and Brian's pleasure at taking his lover flowed between the men. Overcome by the power of it, their bodies shuddered in unison, as if locked in the throes of a mating that seared their souls.

"Dear God." Rush sobbed and clung to Brian as he pounded ever deeper inside his tunnel. He broke down the walls of his past and freed his love for Brian into the charged ether that crackled between them.

His balls drew up, helpless against the onslaught. He came, the wild surge of his semen shot the length of his cock to splatter over his belly and smeared by Brian's belly and chest as he held Rush in his arms.

Unable to control himself, Brian thrust, thrashed, pummeled into Rush, lost in the most primal fuck of his life. Nothing except his need for his cowboy entered his mind, all the blood in his body seemed to gather in his loins, engorging his already-stiff dick.

No use.

"Take me, Rush."

Holding Rush tight, he buried his head in Rush's shoulder and ceased fighting it. The dam broke, his cum rocketed him over the cliff, and from the base of his spine to the tip of his prick, he felt the orgasm take him.

He emptied into Rush's tight, hot channel, sobbed into Rush's neck, and held on as if to let go of the man he loved meant death.

They rocked together, bodies locked, hands caressing. Brian whispered tender words, vowed his love. Rush pledged to spend his life with Brian here at the Double T.

* * *

"Up and at 'em, Officer Russell."

Brian rolled to his side, rubbed his eyes and looked up at Rush, already dressed in a shirt and jeans.

"You're up early." Brian sat on the edge of the bed and dragged on his sweats.

"Had to make sure my man got to work on time. First day is important." Rush handed him a cup of coffee. The mug said, "Cowboy Butts Make Me Nuts."

"You unpacked it for me?" Brian laughed and took a sip.

Rush shook his head. "Your uniform is ready." He pointed to clothes hanging from the closet door.

Brian walked over to them. "You put all the pins on for me," Brian whispered as he touched the badge and traced it with his fingertip.

Rush came up behind him and wrapped his arms around his chest, then snuggled his nose in the space between Brian's neck and shoulder.

"Call me later?"

"Sure. I'll report in at two." He gave Rush a quick kiss on the cheek and headed to the bathroom to get ready.

After his shower, he dressed and found Rush in the kitchen sipping fresh brewed coffee.

"I can't believe it." Brian shook his head.

"What? That I know how to make coffee? All cowboys are trained in the fine art of stewing grounds." Rush's mouth twisted up in a grin.

"Well, yes, but no. That I'm here. That you came out. That I'm finally a cop."

"Me, too. For a minute there, it was touch and go." Rush chuckled as he handed Brian a travel mug of coffee.

"I knew it, you know. The night I first saw you."

"Knew what?"

"That my life was going to change. That something big was about to happen to me." He put on his Stetson and adjusted it.

"God, you look good enough to eat in that uniform." Rush slid into Brian's arms.

"Turns you on?"

"Fuck, yeah. Never knew I had a thing for men in uniforms, but…" He glanced down at the bulge in his jeans. "You got me hard and aching."

Brian groaned and gave Rush a quick caress over the buttons of his fly. "We'll take care of that when I get home."

"Home. I like the sound of that, darlin'," Rush purred and kissed Brian, giving his bottom lip in a gentle nip.

Brian picked up his service belt, swung it around his hips, and buckled it. He checked his Beretta, snapped the guard closed, then walked to the door.

He opened it and stepped through it, then paused. "I'll be home at four."

"I'll be here." Rush gave him a nod.

Brian got in his truck, turned it around, and headed down the road to the highway.

In his rearview mirror, he watched as Rush came out on the porch and took his seat in his chair. Rush raised his arm and gave him a last wave.

Life didn't get better than this.

He had the job he'd always wanted and the cowboy of his dreams.

Brian drove all the way to town with a goofy grin on his face.

Lynn Lorenz

Lynn has been writing all her life, but only recently for publication. She writes a variety of genres besides historicals, including police procedurals, fantasy, paranormal, and contemporary romantic comedy, but enjoys reading suspense and detective stories most of all and wishes more cops would fall in love between their pages.

Born in New Orleans, she has a strong affinity for the South, pralines and po'boys. She's never met food she didn't like, but finds it hard to beat the food she grew up with and constantly craves from N'awlins. Going back occasionally to visit her father who still lives there, her car is often laden with epicurean delights such as Hubig Pies, Barqs in the bottle, Central Groceries' muffalattas and Gambino's pastries.

Graduating with a bachelor's degree in Fine Arts, Lynn is also an artist whose still lifes, life studies, and landscapes are done in acrylic, watercolors, pencil, and pastels. She loves getting away for a week at a time just to paint outdoors.

She has a real job that keeps her busy nine-to-five, but in her spare time she finds it hard to stay away from writing. It keeps her off the streets and out of the bars.

Lynn has two incredible kids, a supportive husband of twenty plus years, and a black lab/Aussie sheep dog mix. She's lived in Katy, Texas, since 1999, where she discovered her love of all things Texan and cowboy, like big hair, boots, and blue jeans. Yeehaw!

Find out more about Lynn by visiting her website: http://www.lynnlorenz.com.

TITLES AVAILABLE In Print from Loose Id®

A GUARDIAN'S DESIRE
Mya

ALPHA
Treva Harte

ALTERED HEART
Kate Steele

CROSSING BORDERS
Z. A. Maxfield

DANGEROUS CRAVINGS
Evangeline Anderson

DARK ELVES: TAKEN
Jet Mykles

DARK ELVES: SALVATION
Jet Mykles

DAUGHTERS OF TERRA:
THE TA'E'SHA CHRONICLES, BOOK ONE
Theolyn Boese

FAITH & FIDELITY
Tere Michaels

FORGOTTEN SONG
Ally Blue

HEAVEN SENT: HELL & PURGATORY
Jet Mykles

LEASHED: MORE THAN A BARGAIN
Jet Mykles

SHARDS OF THE MIND:
THE TA'E'SHA CHRONICLES, BOOK TWO
Theolyn Boese

SLAVE BOY
Evangeline Anderson

SOUL BONDS: COMMON POWERS 1

Lynn Lorenz

THE ASSIGNMENT

Evangeline Anderson

THE BITE BEFORE CHRISTMAS

Laura Baumbach, Sedonia Guillone, and Kit Tunstall

THE BROKEN H

J. L. Langley

THE RIVALS: SETTLER'S MINE 1

Mechele Armstrong

THE TIN STAR

J. L. Langley

Publisher's Note: The print titles listed above were previously released in e-book format by Loose Id®.

Breinigsville, PA USA
18 February 2010
232761BV00001B/62/P